The Summer Demands

THE
SUMMER
DEMANDS

DEBORAH SHAPIRO

CATAPULT  NEW YORK

This is a work of fiction. All of the characters, organizations, and events portrayed in this novel are either products of the author's imagination or used fictitiously.

Published by Catapult
catapult.co

First Catapult printing: 2019

ISBN: 978-1-948226-30-1

Jacket design by Nicole Caputo
Book design by Wah-Ming Chang

Catapult titles are distributed to the trade by
Publishers Group West
Phone: 866-400-5351

Library of Congress Control Number: 2018956398

Printed in the United States of America
10 9 8 7 6 5 4 3 2 1

The summer demands and takes away too much,
But night, the reserved, the reticent, gives more than it takes.

JOHN ASHBERY,
"As One Put Drunk into the Packet-Boat"

The Summer Demands

SPLINTER

Summer, green and still and slightly grainy. The way it is in foreign films from the 1970s and '80s. A lulling, enveloping heat. I had things to do, I swear, written on lists, but those things seemed to get done only if they coincided with the slow, inevitable rhythm of the days. From the couch in the room with the bay window, I would watch those movies, watch young French women who never wore bras move around in philosophically provocative situations, and then I would get up and go outside, go down to the lake, or watch another movie. The days passed into each other without much distinction, dulling all anxiety but heightening a sensitivity. Like walking out of a dark theater into a bright afternoon, one world exchanged for another. Being stunned and not minding it, wanting to hold to an in-between.

I'd started to think of this place as a falling-down estate

owned by a family that had shut it up, fled during a war, leaving us as caretakers. We'd done what we could, David and I, but the playing fields remained overgrown, the tennis, volleyball, and basketball courts all cracked and wild with weeds. The little cove by the lake was filmed with algae. The boathouse, the dining hall, the rec hall, the whitewashed bunks—they were still standing though in need of repair. Most of the bunks here, the original ones, were built in a clearing, in a horseshoe shape around a flagpole. But as the camp had grown, two structures were added at the edge of the woods. It was darker and cooler over there, even on a day in July, the sun bright and blazing before noon, an equatorial light.

I couldn't have said what I was doing over in that part of the property. Taking a different way, maybe, down to the water. Those cabins had always had a secretive quality because they were set apart from the rest of the camp. And when I had been a young camper here, almost thirty years ago, these cabins were where the older girls, in all their mysterious glamour, stayed. If I was alone, I would walk hurriedly by. If there were two or three of us, we would linger, bravely, as if on a dare, waiting to be taken into their world.

The girls were gone now, of course, but something of them remained, some sort of pull, a lasting, palpable atmosphere. A presence. When I heard a sound—a dull thud that repeated, followed by a scraping—I stopped walking and kept listening. The noise was familiar somehow. I made my way around the side of the cabin where the ground rose a little and I could look inside through a screen.

I was sure I hadn't left the shutters open on any of the cabin windows, though now they were propped up with a couple of two-by-fours. And I couldn't remember if the clothesline between these two cabins, that I ducked under, had always been there. But the damp clothes on it—a T-shirt, a black no-wire bra, three pairs of underwear—those were definitely new.

A thud, again. The scraping. And through the screen, a young woman sitting on the dark wood floor, her back toward me. *Shit*, I heard her say—but it didn't appear to be in response to my presence. She stood, moving into the light, holding her right hand in her left, staring at her palm. Long white neck, straight black sweep of hair across her forehead, lanky, a person of lines and edges. I saw then what she'd been doing: playing jacks.

I ran my nails down the screen, gently, a noise that caught her attention. She turned, making me out through the window. No smile, but her face was soft, unalarmed. It made me think she knew me, that she'd seen me before, wandering around, and perhaps had put together some idea of who I was. Which meant she would have been living on our property for a while.

She stepped closer, right up to the screen, looking down at me.

"I have a splinter," she said. "From the floor."

"I have tweezers," I said. "Up at the house."

She nodded, blinked her wide-set eyes, and I went quickly, on a mission, not questioning whether she'd be there when I got back.

We stood in the sun, outside the gloom of the bunk, and

I took her hand to remove the sliver of wood, careful but competent, as if I did this kind of thing for a living. No trouble, anybody would do the same, but the casualness of my gestures already felt like a cover, disguising something I couldn't yet name. She curled her fingers up—her nails painted a dark, galaxy blue—and I let go of her hand abruptly so she wouldn't think I was holding on too long.

Her mouth remained slightly open after thanking me. Then, as if to find something else to do with it, she apologized—*sorry*—though she didn't say what for. She folded her arms and I realized that mine were folded, too, though I wasn't sure who'd mimicked whom.

"You've been living here?" I asked.

"Yeah."

"How long?"

"A couple of months."

"A couple of *months*?"

"Yeah. You probably want me to go?"

I laughed, the question seemed both so innocent and knowing, coupled with a comic timing I wasn't sure she was aware of. I also didn't know what to say—laughter as placeholder or postponement—and out of habit or some deeply internalized patriarchal impulse, I told her I'd have to talk to my husband. She'd seen him? Around?

She'd seen him, she said. And he'd almost seen her, the other day, when she'd been by the rec hall, charging her phone in an exterior outlet.

It occurred to me, then, that she had whole systems in

place. Systems for how to live here without us knowing. How much of us had she seen?

Had she spotted us, that first warm day of the season? From where we'd stood, up at the lodge, you couldn't see to the end of the camp, the point at which the land turned into the lake. We'd never had this much space all to ourselves. This much oxygen. So, we ran. Down across the fields, and I couldn't remember the last time I'd run like that, stumbling, out of breath. Just moving, moving. David liked to run, but he'd been limited until now to city routes. We ran along a wooded path and didn't stop until we reached a patch of grass by the water. We took off only what we needed to and fucked against a tree before we lay on the ground, staring up at the sky—nobody around at all, we thought—and laughed about it, the tree, the fucking. The bark had scratched my back. I had a cramp in my side from running. Better in theory? David asked. Maybe, I answered. Sex in this spot hadn't been a fantasy of mine. But the boathouse . . . We'd do that next, he said.

We didn't, though. Neither of us had brought it up since.

"Are you hungry?" I asked her. It didn't seem like a particularly random or loaded question, just the one that came to me. "Do you want to have lunch?"

"I would, but I have to go to work."

One of us, at least, had a place to be. She had a shift, she said, in a coffee place a couple of miles away in one of the newer shopping centers. I knew the one: brick and glass; sterile, sparse landscaping. Her red collared shirt and her name tag were waiting for her there. She pointed toward the woods—she kept her bike locked to a tree by a path that I hadn't known about. It led out to the road.

"Thanks again," she said, holding up the hand I'd attended to.

"Sure."

Just like that. I hadn't gotten her name. She started to walk off, looked back for a long moment as if she might ask me something, something she'd almost forgotten. Her reserve wasn't affectless, it was alert and ascertaining, and I could still feel it trained on me even as she turned toward the trees. I wanted to say *Wait!* and then I wanted to run—not after her and not away from her, but just to run, to go, to be in motion again. Instead, I stood there, listening to her moving over fallen brush as she made her way through the woods.

WEIRD ENERGY

The car in the drive. David home from work. Some days I couldn't wait for him to break my solitude. Days I could feel myself slipping into a horror story: David goes out into the world and maintains a sane relationship to it while I lose my mind and become this place. Today had been different, though. Someone else had broken my solitude.

When he came in through our front door, I called down to him, suggested we go out for dinner. I practically pushed him back into the car and we went to the one Thai restaurant nearby, along the main street of the village.

We lived in a south shore Massachusetts town, a few historic blocks with street lamps surrounded by houses, Victorians and clapboard Cape Cods, and then, a little farther out, small, cheaply fabricated split-levels and ranches that had replaced dilapidated frame houses sometime in the '50s. American flags. Tracts with gas stations and retail strips, a few sizable stretches of woods that hadn't yet been swallowed up into suburbs, and our camp. Two towns over you could find a yoga studio. We knew people from Boston who'd started families and bought homes outside the city, but they didn't buy here.

I was going to tell David what happened that day, all through dinner I was going to tell him about the young woman whose name I hadn't yet obtained. How I met her and then spent the afternoon going from room to room around our house, wondering what she would make of it. (Had she already been inside it, somehow?) The faded wallpaper, the smooth wood floors, the framed drawings on the mantle, the dark green tile in the bathroom, the stereo and the records. The candlesticks. The plants. She would have had nothing but contempt for our materialism, for all our comforts and calculations. But then I thought, no. She'd made a home, however makeshift, out of her surroundings in the bunk. I'd seen a crate she was using as a nightstand, next to one of the metal bed frames on which she'd laid out a sheet and a blanket. She seemed to have dusted off a wooden dresser, too, and a couple of folded shirts had sat on top. I was going to tell David all of this. But I didn't. Even when he commented on my "weird energy."

"What do you mean?" I asked, though I think I knew.

He looked at me from across the table, silently, curiously, and then glanced toward the room, as if a waiter were about

to bring out a dessert with a candle in it. As if maybe I'd orchestrated a small surprise for him. For an instant I worried
I'd forgotten his birthday, been too preoccupied that day to
remember an occasion and that some disappointment would
cross his face. But that wasn't it. He turned back to me
with a suggestive half-smile, still not sure what I was up to,
though sensing it was something. David: on the taller side,
square-shouldered, but not severe; the roundness of his nose
and softness of his mouth had always struck me somehow as
kind. As first impressions went, he came off as steady, col-
lected. People liked him, and they tended to take him seriously. But if you met his gaze often enough, you'd see this
seriousness called into question by a quick, engaging wit that
flashed in his dark eyes.

"I just can't remember the last time you ordered one of
those iced coffees," he said.

And neither could I—sweet, with condensed milk. A gra-
tuitous, gluttonous drink from my youth. At some point in my
life I'd replaced it with water, an occasional glass of wine. We
could take each other's measure in beverages, David and I, we
had that kind of collective, institutional memory between us.
Despite this, or maybe because of it, I still didn't mention the
young woman.

The warmth of the dark. Moonlight. David was already upstairs when I locked all the doors and the windows on the
first floor. Something I'd rarely thought to do the whole time

we'd been here. I went to bed in only a T-shirt and took it off in the middle of the night, cool and naked beneath the sheet. David slept. Moths opened against the screens of our bedroom windows. I lay there, waiting, waiting, waiting, and I was not sure for what.

Our house had been called the Director's House. White with black shutters, an old farmhouse, though I don't know if there was ever a farm. It was where my great-aunt Esther and her husband, Joe, had lived for years while they ran the camp. Esther and Joe had been city kids: triple-decker houses and apartment buildings, lunch counters, shoe shops, bakeries with rye bread and challah, kosher butchers, *shul*. The Mystic River, smokestacks, crowds, streetcars, and Revere Beach. They'd grown up in Chelsea, a large, tightly knit community of working- and lower-middle-class Jewish immigrants from Eastern Europe. Second- and third-generation children moved out and up to the Boston suburbs but Esther and Joe and their families hadn't yet prospered enough to leave.

One summer, through the efforts of a charitable Jewish organization, Joe and Esther had the chance to go away to camp. This was part of a program whose unstated mission was to foster comfort in nature and self-defense skills. It was 1945. At fifteen, Esther and Joe had never been away from home, never really been more than a few miles from their neighborhood, from their many brothers and sisters, from the clatter of city life. They knew dirt but they'd never held soil in their hands.

When Esther and Joe—resolutely urban, nurtured by density, neurosis, and the Great Depression—discovered the woods, they never wanted to leave.

Across an asphalt road, the one real road in the camp, sat the Lodge, a ramshackle one-story building constructed in the same style as the Director's House, painted white with a layer of black trim curling and flaking to reveal a faded pine green. When we'd first arrived, David and I, pulling off a winding rural road and into a half-circular drive, I saw the lodge at the center of the curve and I practically leaped out of the truck we'd loaded up with our possessions, ushering myself in through a partially unhinged screen door, into a world of linoleum floors, dust on heavy wooden desks in a room used for administrative purposes, then hurricane lamps and two sofas—one floral, one patchy gold velour—in a room that had been designated as the Lounge. I was entering a photograph of my own past, my family's past. Yellowed posters bearing the faces of imprisoned Soviet dissidents were still tacked along one wall. In the '80s, when I had come here as a girl, we had sung songs about them, singing for their release. I didn't know what had become of them since. But David did. That one, he said, finally emigrated to America and became a neocon lobbyist. That one died after being exiled to Siberia.

How do you know that? I asked.

How do you not? he said.

•

I thought the girl might have cleared out in the night. That the bunk would be bare, as if she'd never been there at all and I'd imagined the whole thing.

I knocked softly on the door, accommodating, polite. She had trespassed on our private property, but I didn't seem to mind. Even though all I really knew of her was that she played jacks, supposedly worked as a barista, had a cell phone and bike, hair like a dramatic brushstroke, and a quiet but sure way of setting up her space. That she was a cause, perhaps, of the strange, subtle coiling feeling taking place inside me. That she was alert, ascertaining. I knocked and she answered. She came out onto the wood-plank steps in the bright morning wearing peach-colored sunglasses with mirrored lenses, so all I saw for a moment was my own reflection, trying to look like I wasn't trying too hard, my shoulder-length brown hair piled on my head, threadbare T-shirt, cutoffs that were loose, unraveling. Then she came into focus. She was a little taller than me, and thinner, so that a kind of buff-colored canvas karate pant looked good on her, as did the standard red polo shirt she had to put on for work. She wore it oversized, revealing the length of her collarbone. Her hair was damp. She must have figured out how to turn the water on for the plumbing in the bunk. Resourceful girl.

"I know, I should go," she said, pushing the sunglasses up into her wet hair, a gesture that struck me as disarming; those mirrored lenses were like a shield. And mostly because she wasn't putting me in the position of being the uptight, incurious person telling her to leave, I wanted her to stay.

"Well, you don't have to. I mean, not right away." I leaned on the unsteady railing of the stoop. I didn't want to keep shifting but that's what I did, while she rested against the door frame of the bunk, at ease, like she would take whatever I said in stride. Like she was used to taking everything in stride, or at least pretending to.

"Did you talk to your husband?"

"What?" I said. "Oh." A small, embarrassed laugh. "No, actually. Not yet."

"Stella," she said, showing me her hand, the one I'd held the day before, and then extending it.

"Emily." I shook her hand and then wondered, again, if I'd released it too soon or too late. "Are you off to work?"

"I have a little time before then."

"Oh. Well, do you want to go for a walk or something?" It was strange, ostensibly having all the power here but feeling that I was the one taking a risk. A sense of relief, a stirring to life, when she said okay.

We walked, out past the cluster of the rec hall, the old arts-and-crafts building, and a large storage shed of moldering athletic equipment. Into the full sun of the basketball court, the nets on the baskets having mostly disintegrated on the rusting rims. Into a shaded path that led to a bench by a stone wall. She seemed to know this place as well as I did.

She'd grown up close to here, she told me, not too far from Plymouth. She should have had a Boston accent, misplaced r's, drawn-out vowels; hints of it came through in a word or two, but mostly she sounded like she was from any place, no place.

Plymouth, where the pilgrims eventually landed the *May-flower* in 1620, where actors dressed up as seventeenth-century colonists at a reenactment village. You could visit them in their thatched-roof homes, and they would try to inhabit their time, telling you about blacksmithing or cutting hay, while also having a contemporary sensitivity and awareness of what that time would become. I had been there once on a school field trip. Stella had been there many times, she told me, and she'd even worked in the gift shop one summer.

"People would always try to get the actors to break character," she said. "You know, say something about modern life or drop their English accents. Not just kids, parents, too. Teacher chaperones, even. It always seemed like a weird thing to do. Weird and mean. Like everyone knows it's an act, you've bought a ticket to see the act and be part of it and then you're trying to get the actors to mess up, you're trying to get someone to be bad at their job so you can go 'aha!' Or something. Like what kind of satisfaction do you get out of that?"

"When you put it that way, it does seem mean and weird."

"Just let them do their job, you know?"

"Yeah."

"It's like, I do my job and I don't give a shit but I *do* give a shit. I try to get people's names right. And then you mess up and they take a picture of their name spelled wrong on the cup and post it online. My ex used to do that. Her name is Alice. How can you really get that wrong, right? One time she ordered a coffee someplace and they wrote 'Salad' on it and she was like, *what the fuck* and laughing. But what if your name *is* Salad or something? Maybe that's what they heard and they just didn't want to offend her."

When Stella let out a what-the-fuck laugh recalling her ex-girlfriend Alice's what-the-fuck laugh, she smiled wide and radiant, and I found myself smiling, too. But then, at the thought of her ex, maybe, she pressed her lips shut, puffed her cheeks, and then blew out the breath. I stopped smiling, too.

"I need a job," I said, because she'd brought up the subject of work, and asking about Alice, even though she'd also brought that up, felt like prying somehow. And I didn't want to appear at all flustered by the knowledge that she liked women. Because why, really, should I have been flustered? "I'm looking for a job."

"What kind of job? What do you do?"

What did I do? I walked around here a lot. I'd tried to garden. I went for swims. I took a canoe out onto the lake. I took pictures of the neglected spaces, the empty dining hall, the long tables I'd once sat at now pushed against the wall, the industrial oven shut like a gigantic, ancient mouth, orange life jackets faded by the sun that found its way into the boathouse, massive cobwebs, secret messages scrawled in marker on rafters in the cabins. Names I knew and names I didn't. Lost girlhood. There was so much long-gone girlhood around here. Scrawled hearts on the walls. Doggerel about boys. About body parts, burps, and farts. Palimpsests of so many summers past. It was going to be a project. There was an old enlarger up at the lodge and a ventilated space that had once been used as a dark-room when photography had been offered as a camp activity. I would buy new chemicals, develop these photographs, maybe write text to go with them. It could be a book?

It was true that I was looking for work, I explained. I told her about the job postings I scrolled through each day with descriptions that all read like advertising copy for an extreme sports drink. "Are you ready to kick ass and take names?" *No.* "We believe work is play. Have you got game?" *I'm not sure.* "Do you have a passion for juices?" *I like juice, but no, I wouldn't say passion.* Still, I hit send on my résumé. Every click showed me my age. Thirty-nine. I wouldn't have hired me if I were these people.

"I'm not exactly sure what it is that I do," I told her. "I inherited this camp and we came here thinking we would redo it, make it into a kind of resort, but that hasn't really worked out."

"No?"

"Well, I don't know. You're our guest, I suppose. Guest number one."

She and Alice had actually come here together, she said, in late May. But they'd broken up. Alice went back to Cambridge. She was going to be a senior at Harvard in September. Stella was going to be what she'd always been, a townie. Her word.

Stella laughed again, from her chest and with her shoulders.

"Who the fuck has a passion for juices?" she said.

Stella had asked me what it was that I did. In what seemed more and more like another life, I had been a journalist. Or maybe "a writer of service journalism" was a better way to put it. I talked to people who wanted to talk, who had something to publicize, and punched that up into a story. But I wasn't the best at coaxing information from someone who wasn't already eager to share. When I'd started working at a newspaper, just out of college, I imagined I might do it for a few years and then apply to graduate school—a writing program, maybe a film program—but I never did. It turned out I liked my job, or I liked the way it kept me from interrogating my own ambition. For a while, anyway. If you don't try—if you tell yourself you can't try because certain circumstances prevent you—then you can't fail. And there was still a gruff, ink-stained glamour to the profession at the time I got into it. The hard-boiled investigative reporter, Gene, who leaned back in his swivel chair and grumbled at whoever was on the other end of the line: "Look, you're either a source or a target. What do you want to be?" He liked me because I liked him and I knew who Rosalind Russell was, I had seen *His Girl Friday* more than once. But I remember thinking, *Is that all it takes? Knowing the right references to flatter the vanity of this middle-aged man?* It went some distance, but it wasn't all it took, of course. Gene accepted a buyout two years before my job was eliminated and then the paper essentially became a listings guide.

I moved into public relations work, in New York and then in Chicago, and for a while I had enough hustle to disguise my lack of conviction, but eventually people—clients—could tell. One of them, who considered herself a friend, encouraged me to go with her to a gathering at a wine bar for "professional women." It was the kind of event where you couldn't make a joke about being an "amateur woman." I went home and felt terrible about myself.

But what kept me from feeling too terrible was that I had already shifted my focus elsewhere. David and I were trying to have a child. I would be a parent and—problem solved—that would be my primary identity. I knew better than to talk about it this way, for any number of political, cultural, and psychological reasons. I knew, from conversations with my friend Liz, a mother of two young girls, that it didn't really work that way, even if you wanted it to. But, I secretly thought, I'm not Liz. Liz is not me. And I was right about that, at least. I wasn't Liz. I wasn't able, it seemed, to have one child, let alone two.

We had sought out fertility specialists. We had sat in waiting rooms exchanging expectant looks of hope and vulnerability with the people waiting with us. I remember one stylish, fox-faced woman whose appearance suggested expertise and sophistication, that she knew how to move through the world, how to do everything successfully, everything, that is, but this. Her tight air of determination initially struck me as a caricature, until one day I realized I was setting my mouth in the same grim little line.

But then. But then! All of the science, the shots, the waiting, the failing, the trying again. It worked. It actually worked. I felt it almost immediately, my body recalibrating itself, reshaping itself. My body forcing my guarded mind to accept that this was happening. I'd read—God, I'd read so much—that you wouldn't need maternity clothes for a few months at least, but though I could fit into the pants I owned, they all felt too restrictive. It was as if, on a cellular level, I had been enlarged overnight. Like my blood had thickened. I wanted space and ease. I wanted soft, stretchy waistbands from the get-go. And I was exhausted all the time. *No shit*, said Liz, when I called her. *Your body is making another body.* And David and I marveled at how uncanny that was. What my body could do. My body could make another body! My body could even get my hopes up.

You would feel betrayed, wouldn't you, by someone who got your hopes up only to dash them. You would think that at best, that someone was recklessly naive, and at worst, extremely cruel. At fourteen weeks in, our doctor couldn't find a heartbeat. I'd had what's called a missed miscarriage. One of the few things I hadn't read about, couldn't bring myself to read about. And so, though I vaguely knew what a D&C was, I hadn't comprehended that I would need a procedure to remove everything that had been growing inside of me, the body that my body, so recklessly naive, had been making. For three months, I had felt so powerful in a purely biological, unthinking way. And then, for no particular reason anyone could determine, my body became a tender, faulty thing and all I could do was think.

I didn't quite know how to make sense of time, after we lost the baby. I kept organizing my life, my hours and days, around something that no longer existed in time: *This is when I would have started to feel it kicking, this is when I would have given birth.* David told me he did the same, but I did it for longer. I did it for so much longer I felt I had to start keeping it a secret, because if anyone knew, they would—out of concern for my sanity—try to take that compulsion away from me, too.

When our child would have been about three months old, my great-aunt Esther died of heart failure, of age essentially, and I learned she'd made me her beneficiary. She'd left me the whole camp, with no instructions or provisions on what to do with it. For more than fifty years, a couple hundred girls had come to Camp Alder every July and August, including me. But for the last fifteen years or so, it had sat empty. Uncle Joe had died, and Esther, in her final years, had moved to an assisted-living facility.

We'd have to sell it. We lived, at the time, halfway across the country, and what would we do with an old camp? The question started to resolve itself only when I asked myself why we lived halfway across the country. Why still. We had gone to Chicago when David was offered a career-making opportunity. But we had no family there. And by then I had no real job. And David's career-making opportunity had become a source of growing bitterness about the corporatized direction his organization, an architecture firm that was supposed to specialize in housing for low-income populations and the homeless, was heading in. He said he wished he worked with his hands again. He had spent summers in school doing construction.

An idea took hold and I laid it out. We would move. To the camp. We would make it into a resort. Camp for adults, it was something of a trend at the time. I'd heard of ones in the Hudson Valley and Wisconsin. A place for companies that considered themselves forward-thinking to hold retreats, for the kind of weddings that became weeklong events. Why couldn't we do this? Maybe, in the off-season, we could host a residency for artists. We would spruce it up just enough, add a few elevated touches: nice sheets, striped wool blankets, interesting but unobtrusive enameled fixtures. Stationery for guests to write letters home. The bunks would be cozy. The dining hall awash in elegant light. Half Adirondacks lodge, half turn-of-the-twentieth-century Austrian sanatorium. And the food. The food! We would have a marvelous chef. Some friend of a friend who was superb but underappreciated. We would grow our own ingredients. I would learn about greens and root vegetables. I would buy overalls and wear them.

"That sounds like a fantasy," said David. "An Internet-fueled fantasy. And kind of cynical."

"And?"

I admitted I no longer knew what cynicism was and if there was a point when it doubled back on itself and became belief. But I was convinced we wouldn't be building an exclusive enclave, we'd be building a welcoming microcosm. I put it this way to David, to dovetail with his principled view of the world. If it all went well, perhaps we could even apply for grants, establish some sort of partnership where we provided housing and helped people—homeless families, refugees—get back on their feet.

"That's not really how it works," he said. But there was something encouraging in his smile, a pleasure in seeing a spark in me he'd thought was gone.

"Look who's cynical now."

I had a goal, a new possibility, a different way to keep track of time. I populated spreadsheets. I determined the proposition was risky but possible. I convinced David. We let our lease run out, sold off some of our furniture, packed up the rest in a truck, and set off for New England in the winter, leaving one cold climate for another. We'd counted on red tape in getting the proper permits and licensing and loans. We anticipated the surfacing of unseen structural problems. We had thought that time plus money plus will could result in achievement, but it turned out we didn't have the right amount of each variable to resolve the equation.

The clouds threatened rain all morning, and when it came, sheets of it hitting the shutters, Stella and I were in her bunk, flashlights and an old lamp I'd found for her in the lodge glowing against the gloom. I'd turned on the bunk's electric supply for her. We were playing jacks, the set she'd found on a shelf. She'd had to look up the object of the game on her phone. She needed to remind me, too, but though I'd forgotten the rules, the weight of the tarnished, pointed metal pieces was so familiar in my palms. The glinting green rubber ball hadn't deteriorated at all. We scoured the floor for rough spots—there would be no splinters today.

Her nails were still that galactic blue, though it had come off a little. Time to repaint, she said. So that's what we did when we'd had enough of jacks. She had two bottles of polish, the blue and a dark, glossy red. Crimson, she said, choosing for me. She expertly used only a minimum of polish remover on a cotton ball and then brushed on a fresh coat of the navy lacquer. I struggled to look as skilled as Stella. It took me forever to do one hand, the color going all over my fingers because I'd had no practice. I rarely did this.

"Here," she said, taking my other hand, in a competent, caring, practiced manner, like I'd first taken hers, when removing that splinter, and she placed it on the floor in front of her. But there was also a tenderness in her touch. And—I don't think I was imagining it—an electricity. Something transformative, too: In no time, my fingers seemed to belong to a woman with dark brows and cutting cheekbones, holding an apple to her open mouth, in a silk dress and the highest heels, in front of a camera lens somewhere in Paris in the 1980s.

"That's totally your color," she said.

"Really?"

"I mean, it's the only other color I have. But yeah."

She looked from my hands to my face and then my neck as if she were answering a question she'd asked herself.

"I think I have something that belongs to you," she said, and she got up, opened the top drawer of her dresser, and turned around, holding out a gold necklace, a chain with a small disc imprinted with an "E." It shone out of the low light. David had given it to me as a birthday present years back and I'd lost it a month or so before. By the water, I'd thought, though I couldn't be sure.

"Yes, that's mine." I was relieved to see it again, but that relief didn't squash a wrenching in my gut and a tightening I could feel across my face.

"I found it down by the lake. I figured it could have been anybody's though probably yours. But at the time, I didn't know how to return it to you without either letting you know I was here or totally creeping you out. Like, I mean, if I'd left it visibly on your porch or something, you'd be like, *what the fuck, who put that there*, right?"

"Right. Yeah."

"Here," she said, and because my nails were still drying, she moved behind me to put it around my neck, brushing my hair to the side. She didn't linger when she hooked the clasp, she efficiently performed a task, like a hairstylist or a doctor or any other professional who might have cause to touch the back of your neck. But I'd never before replayed to myself—as I did on my way back to the house, when the rain let up a little—the motions, the positioning, the feel of any hairstylist or doctor who'd ever touched the nape of my neck.

"It's so pretty on you," she'd said, stepping around to look at me. And I'd lowered my gaze to the disc hanging around my neck, so I didn't have to look at her looking at me.

Back at the house, I didn't even get out of my raincoat, I went straight up to my room, taking the stairs in twos, to examine the tray where I kept a few bracelets, and with my glossy nails—polish made them feel different, more object-like—I opened a velvet-lined box. I didn't own much expensive jewelry but what I had, a couple of pendants, an emerald ring from Aunt Esther, was all still there, exactly where I remembered it being. Stella was honest, I reassured myself. If there was dishonesty here, it was my own, I thought, out of breath, standing there with water dripping off my raincoat.

Later, David asked about my day. Any job prospects?

I told him I had a lead on something. A lie. I knew we'd eventually need another income if we wanted to keep living as we were and continue to pay off our medical bills (how could there be more medical bills? still?) and the debt we'd taken on to finance our plan for reviving this place. But I didn't want to think too hard about it right now, about my employability or how necessary, how urgent it might be for me to find work.

I put my hands on the kitchen table, daring David to know something was up, but he didn't notice, or he pretended not to notice, what I'd spent a good deal of the rest of that afternoon doing: admiring my crimson manicure. Stella was honest, and she'd said it was my color, so it was.

"How was your day?" I asked him.

Work was a series of disappointing client meetings, he told me, and I tried to be interested and consoling, because he'd found a job when we couldn't make a go of the resort, because he worked hard, because I loved him, because he was starting to resent me, because I was pleased with my nails.

When we finished our dinner of pasta and tomato sauce from a jar, I washed the dishes with a sense of purpose. I'd started living according to a certain arithmetic: If I did enough dishes, David couldn't resent me as much. I took a glass vase out of a cupboard, rinsed it, too, and placed it on the counter, thinking that the next day, I would fill it with flowers. I would set a table. I would open a cookbook and make us a proper meal.

David sat on the living room couch in semidarkness, looking at his phone.

"David, David, David," I said.

He held on to his phone longer than he should have, out of habit, but before this could depress me, I took it from him, standing over him. He looked up, called back to a place that, out of habit, we hadn't been for far too long. Then he took my hand, pulling me toward him.

"I like your nails."

"Thank you."

"You found it," he said, reaching up to touch the gold disc resting below my collar bone.

I climbed on top of him. There was nothing covering the bay window in that room. It faced a backyard that turned into brush. I kept looking at the glass as if I might see someone outside, but all I got was my own reflection.

Stella was golden in the sun. We lay on towels in the sand and she glittered, smooth and tan, after we'd been swimming in the lake. I had on a form-fitting, long-sleeve shirt, made of bathing-suit material, and though it protected me from getting burned, from ultraviolet damage, I wondered what the point was. My skin didn't look like Stella's did, like it sought out a two-piece in a kind of mandated-by-nature symbiosis. It might have, when I was younger, but I hadn't known then to

appreciate it. Or I knew—the world was always telling you—
but I couldn't comprehend it, I didn't feel it. And maybe I
had never been like Stella. I had thought she must put something in her short, straight black-brown hair, a balm or a spray,
to make it fall so sharply around her face, with the sweep of
bangs angled to the outer corner of her eye. But it naturally
dried that way. Falling just so.

In this effortlessness, she reminded me of the older girls at
camp who had fascinated me when I was eight, nine, ten. Those
girls were visions. Part mothers, part sisters, heroines, idols.
They were sixteen, seventeen, eighteen. Some were thin, some
muscular, some chubby. Their features had come into fullness
and it seemed like they could never be dulled and they were all
equally beautiful. But I can see that's only true in retrospect.
At the time, we younger girls absorbed—as if by osmosis, nobody ever said a word—the workings of an intricate caste system. We understood there was a hierarchy even if we couldn't
have said what it was or how, exactly, you came to occupy your
place. At the top, the girls could be quiet or loud, careful or
bold, academic achievers or average-grade getters, from wealthy
Westchester or one of the less affluent towns outside Boston,
attending camp with the assistance of a scholarship fund Esther and Joe had established. There were no specific criteria you
could point to. But we all knew where each of the older girls
stood. They had their favorites, too. Younger girls to whom they
were especially kind or attentive, the shining girls in whom they
saw themselves, and occasionally the girls they thought were less
fortunate, whom they could pity with their charitable hearts.

At the end of each season a themed banquet was held. Under the Sea, On Safari. The bunk of older girls who put it together each year would dress accordingly. The rest of us would wear our best outfits and, for about a half an hour before the dinner started, the girls who'd come to camp with disposable or compact cameras took pictures of each other. An exercise in exclusion, in documenting who was part of your group and who didn't make it into the frame.

When I was ten, the banquet theme was Outer Space, and my friend Wendy and I got dressed early and went to the bunk of older girls who were putting the finishing touches on their costumes. They loved Wendy, with her freckles, her sweetness, and her athletic ability. They told her how cute she looked, while one of them braided her hair. I sat quietly on the bed next to her, wearing a pink shirt Wendy had let me borrow. It had a perforated mesh pocket, above which was stitched the name of a popular French label. I wore my own denim skirt, brand: unknown, provenance: discount store.

An older girl who had dressed as an alien—in a plastic headband with springs stuck into glitter-coated Styrofoam spheres—noticed me and said, "Hey, sweetie." A loaded term of endearment; I thrilled to it even as I intuited she didn't know my name. "Is that top yours?"

The question wasn't a question. She knew, somehow, that it wasn't mine and wanted me to know that. I smiled strangely and shook my head, wanting nothing more than to dash out of there and back to my bunk to change, but I had nothing to change into. "Well, you look nice," she said. I had never before been complimented in a way that seemed designed to make me ashamed, with no real understanding of what I was being shamed for or what it was I sat there feeling ashamed of.

I'd turned onto my stomach, resting my head on my folded arms, my hair falling over my face, and Stella, sitting on her towel now, lifted a piece of it, like a curtain—*you there?*—and I looked up at her through my hair, which was still as dark as it had always been, only stray grays here and there. I shifted so all I saw was Stella against the trees and sky.

"Who cuts your hair?" I asked her.

"Alice, most recently. She was really good at it. I've been doing it myself but it doesn't turn out as well."

For a while I had wanted the story of how she and Alice met, and now Stella decided to tell me. She'd been living in Boston. Somerville, to be exact. Working at a music venue and a different coffee place. The music venue tended to attract college kids, and one night, at a show, Alice arrived and she kept looking at Stella and sometimes Stella would make eye contact in return.

Alice had darkly made-up eyes. She wore a deep green slip dress and a fuzzy purple jacket when everyone else was in black jeans and T-shirts. Stella supposed Alice thought herself intimidating, and Stella wasn't particularly interested in intimidation. But after the show, Alice came over and said she had to talk to her because the two of them were the only ones there with amazing hair. It meant something, didn't she think? Stella wasn't sure but she supposed it wasn't nothing.

Alice came from New York. Brooklyn Heights. In her

junior year at Harvard, after taking a couple of semesters off. Studying comparative literature. Stella liked that these facts, as Alice presented them to her, weren't accompanied by the kind of embarrassment that rich girls so often expressed when they spoke to her—as if her presence, her existence, shamed them. Alice didn't pretend she was poor or that she was unaware of what wealth did for her. Alice was accustomed to having choices, and in this way, she chose Stella.

It didn't bother Stella at first. Alice's glamour and bossiness weren't alien to Stella. They were, in fact, like a more fully realized and externalized version of qualities Stella knew she, Stella, inwardly possessed. Or maybe, just maybe, Stella would occasionally think in the months to come, she was the more fully realized and externalized of the two and Alice was only playing that role.

"I don't know what I'm trying to say," said Stella. "But do you know what I mean?"

I propped myself up on my elbows and stared down at my towel, gold and moss green, from a set left in Esther and Joe's linen closet. I think she may have meant that Alice's glamour and bossiness was based on habit and insecurity, while her own ability to meet and to match that glamour and bossiness, when she so wished, derived from self-respect. And Stella had entranced Alice in this way, perhaps—through her aura of self-respect.

"Alice thought I was interesting."

"You are interesting."

"No, but interesting like a specimen. Like something to

study," Stella said. "At first I thought that was our thing. Like we were our own kind of project. We weren't just, like, *a couple*. We were creating something that gave us purpose. Only, she could keep going with it in her mind, keep spinning it out, like our attraction was a philosophical game or something for her, and I didn't care enough about that game, not in the way she did."

"Maybe you cared about something else more."

"A lot of the time I could already see myself as someone she would look back on years from now. So maybe I wasn't totally in it either. We were going to come here together for the summer. I'd told her about this place."

"You were going to summer here."

Stella gave me a smile like I'd seen children give: guilty, amused, expecting to be rewarded for their mischief.

"Yeah, we were going to be the kind of people who summer somewhere. As a joke, but we'd actually go, so, not a joke. But she got this fellowship and decided to stay at school."

Stella reached for her backpack, pulling out her phone to show me a photo of Alice. Her long, thick hair pulled back in an undone braid, like a nineteenth-century woman on the wall of the Musée d'Orsay. All entitled, voluptuous composure and insolence.

I asked Stella if she and Alice were still in contact.

"I don't know. Not really. But she's still in my phone, you know? People think I don't give a fuck about things. Something about my face, I guess. Or maybe I don't give a fuck about what they need me to give a fuck about. But my point is,

I generally do give a fuck about things. And I think that was a problem for Alice. That I gave a fuck about things she didn't. I'm sure she's deleted me. I'm long gone from her world."

"I doubt that."

"Well, you haven't met Alice. But yeah, I get that maybe it's easier, for me, to think that she can be so absolute about it being over."

"What did you give a fuck about that she didn't?"

"I don't know. People? Feelings? I'm not even sure she liked me, as a human being. I think she liked me as a model for some kind of nonambition. And like I was a weird novelty to her in that way. If I had ambition it was a kind that didn't correspond to what she'd been raised with, that didn't even understand itself in those terms. I mean, just because I don't go to Harvard doesn't mean I don't want to do anything with my life. I don't want to be a barista forever. But it's all right for now, you know?"

I said that I understood that. How ambition was complicated. When you wanted something badly, you could become invested in the wanting. And then when that wanting didn't result in the imagined outcome, or maybe even when it did, you were left in a situation where you had to give up the state of wanting you'd gotten so used to. Who were you, in a way, when the wanting was gone?

I was thinking out loud, I suppose. Voicing some ongoing conversation I'd been having with myself.

"You mean this camp, not being able to make it into a resort or whatever?" Stella asked.

"No, I guess I'm thinking more about how we got to this place, how we even ended up here at Alder."

Stella had been digging her heels in the sand, creating shallow channels, moats. She stopped for a moment.

"Did you think about trying to revive it as a camp for kids?" she asked.

"No."

"Why? Do you hate children?"

She hadn't expected me to laugh.

"I mean—"

"I don't hate kids."

At twenty-two, she was closer to being a child, in years, than she was to being my age.

"No, I get it," Stella said. "I don't want to have kids."

"Ever?"

"Yeah. Why? Why would you do that to yourself and to another human being?"

"It's that bad?"

"No." Her consideration of the subject played out across her face—slightly raised brows, skewed, pensive mouth. "But sometimes. Yeah."

"Well, you never know, you might change your mind."

She nodded, conceding but unbelieving. As if the concepts of reversal and ambivalence were possible but abstract. Like she could only place herself in them the way she could place herself on an imagined ice floe in Antarctica.

"Do you want to have kids?" she asked me.

There was something so straightforward about Stella's

question—as if she had no idea how loaded such a question could be. Coming from her, it was a simple inquiry, which somehow made it possible for me to answer. I sat up, wrapping my arms around my knees, facing the water and the dock, with Stella in my peripheral vision.

"We tried. I always wanted a child in a kind of abstract way, like someday it'd be nice to have a family. I never imagined it in great detail but I sort of just always saw it as happening one day, though I never had the biological urgency some women talk about. But there's this point where everyone around you is having kids. And maybe it sounds shallow and wrong but that made me want it in this even stronger, more immediate way. Like I'd be left behind. I'd be missing out. So we started trying. And it wasn't happening. And then I had a miscarriage. And." And and and.

"I'm sorry." She brought her hand to my forearm, her blue fingertips resting on my wrist.

And then I found myself apologizing. I barely knew her. I shouldn't have been telling her all of this.

"We might keep trying," I said, brightly, like I'd made her sad and now I needed to cheer her up. "You know, with more fertility treatments and all that. Maybe adoption. We can't really afford more trying, though. It just seems like . . . like a lot now."

I thought of my brother's son, of visiting their house a couple of years earlier, without David for some reason, and my nephew was five and couldn't sleep and he appeared, by the side of the guest room bed, carrying a pillow on which he'd

arranged an assortment of stuffed animals. Two of his cher-
ished "Lolos," what he interchangeably called these bears with
formless velour handkerchief bodies, a small plush owl, and a
fox he'd considerately picked out for me. He asked if he could
sleep in this bed with me and I said sure, thinking that my
brother wouldn't approve but that I couldn't refuse him. He got
under the covers and I reached over to touch his cheek and then
his so-thin shoulder and, already more than half asleep, he took
my arm into the fold and held it close to himself, as if it were
another one of his animals. It wasn't entirely unlike the tender
way Stella had taken my hand in hers when she painted my
nails, or the way her fingertips had rested on my wrist just now.

"Alice would say something like, I don't know, she'd say
we make our own families. Or like, what even is family? She'd
reduce it to something that's not worth having. A social con-
struct that's dangerous and divisive."

"Why is she still in your phone?"

"I don't know." She smiled, shrugged. "Why haven't you
told your husband I'm here?"

In an office in the lodge, the old microphone of the PA system
still sat out on a large wooden desk. When I'd gone to camp
here, every night at lights-out, a counselor would sing "Taps"
into it. *All is well. Safely rest. God is nigh.*

The one summer I worked there as a counselor, my closest
friend was a girl my age named Berrie Lerner. She had wildly
curly hair and gray eyes and a boyfriend back home she was

going to break up with because she couldn't stop thinking about John, one of the boys around our age who worked on the kitchen staff, whom she had been with all July. I was with Stuart, another "kitchen guy," as they were called, and the four of us would go down to the lake some nights and go swimming or just sit in the sand, or on the low concrete retaining wall, and fool around. Stuart and I quickly came to an unspoken understanding that we liked each other, liked each other's body, but that neither of us fascinated the other. Berrie and John fascinated us. When the four of us were together, we were spectators and Berrie and John were the show.

When it was Berrie's turn to sing "Taps," her voice, a steady contralto, would come through the PA system strong and clear but also soft. A voice to tuck you in and kiss your cheek. Berrie thought the last line went *God is night.* I could have corrected her when she came out and we sat on the steps with our flashlights, the heat of the day replaced by a coolness that required a sweatshirt. We'd be quiet for a while before we began to whisper about the girls or something that had happened that day or what we would do on our day off, how high school and our towns seemed so far away. Berrie would make a pronouncement about field hockey or blow jobs, in a you-know-how-it-is way, like a jaded forty-something divorcee, and then she would giggle or moan and—*oh, shit*—remember where we were and what time it was and lower her voice. God was nigh. God was night.

·

Stella had left me a note on a piece of blue scrap paper, slipped through the mail slot in the front door of my house and onto the small kilim rug in the front hall, sometime after David headed out in the morning. She would be back this afternoon, said the note. We could go boating, maybe? She included her cell phone number and signed it: S. Her handwriting was girlish, looping, pleased with itself, more feminine and bubbly than I would have expected. It didn't have the ageless quality of a certain kind of cursive that used to be taught—the penmanship of Aunt Esther, script that you could read pages and pages of. Irrationally, I used to think my own handwriting would evolve, as I got older, to resemble Aunt Esther's hand. But it remained crabbed and illegible.

I could've tossed the note—I had her number now—but instead I took it upstairs and buried the blue paper in my nightstand drawer. And then I waited. I went online and read an article on how to build a professional network and counted this as a productive use of my time.

I looked at old pictures of Esther and Joe. I'd come across a shoebox full of photos in the house and an album in the lodge—green imitation leather, a three-ring binder of yellowed adhesive pages covered in flimsy plastic. In the early '70s: Some windy day. Esther in her trench coat, her dark, wavy hair pinned up under a thin scarf tied at her chin, her burgundy leather pocketbook. Joe in his belted trousers, his undershirt visible beneath his collar, his shirtsleeves rolled to reveal his still muscular, hairy arms. In the late '40s: Esther in a dark floral silky dress, patent leather heels with cracks and creases in them, Joe in a suit and tie. The '50s: In front of their house (our house) where saplings had just been planted.

Esther and Joe never had children, though they'd tried. This fact had occurred to me before, vaguely, but I never felt the force of it, the force of that absence, until I experienced it myself. Until we'd entered into that world of biological chance, until pregnancy became something I sought rather than sought to avoid, I'd mostly thought childlessness was a choice. Or I hadn't given it much thought either way. The final time I saw Esther was at a bar mitzvah shortly after I'd been through another failed IVF round—the last fertility treatment I believed I could endure (though it turned out I would endure one more). She'd asked about my life, the two of us at a table, David buttonholed into small talk elsewhere in the reception room, and I told her the truth. How could I not? We had been each other's favorite in our family. And somewhat hunched-back now, wearing a black robelike dress, she reminded me of a large, friendly owl blinking through her thick glasses. Surely she had some wisdom to impart.

"All the people we knew," she said, "all they did was talk and talk and talk, but not about that. Or they would talk about it happening, like gossip, but they would never talk about it with *you*. The only person I could talk to was Joe, because it was his loss, too. But even then, there was a loss that was only mine, and I couldn't keep losing."

"I can't either," I said. I took in the dance floor, where my cousin's thirteen-year-old son and his friends had gathered, some of them obnoxious, some tentative, a few spontaneously giving themselves over to the music.

Esther placed her bony, spotted hand on mine, gently patting it first, and then squeezing.

About a year later, I learned she'd left the camp to me. For as long as I could remember, I'd seen Esther and Joe as an iconoclastic duo that had sneaked away from, but still had strong ties to, the neighborhood they came from. Their families. Their brothers and sisters. Esther had lost two older brothers in the Second World War and Joe had lost one, yet there were still so many of them. Esther had four other siblings and Joe had six. There were so many of them that none of them, not even my grandfather, my father's father, were entirely real to me. Except for Esther and Joe, the youngest in their families, a half-generation younger than their oldest siblings. I knew most of them only as a small child, and the women were all one woman to me: folds of powdery skin, curled silver hair, Bakelite jewelry, enormous breasts that could smother you. The men: out-of-shape heavyweight boxers, cologne, ill-fitting suits, thinning straight hair or wild wiry locks. They were like illustrations in one of my picture books. I associated all of them with deli platters, Jordan almonds, those toothpicks with the crinkly cellophane flourish on top, Yiddish.

We might have lived in their house and inhabited their camp but David and I were not Esther and Joe. We didn't have an extended family of campers and staff. We had—I had—Stella.

•

The paddles and lifejackets we got from the boathouse. The canoe was already down by the water. Stella sat in the front and I took the back. We made our way through weeds and a tangle of lily pads—the rhythm of the strokes returned to me easily and Stella knew it too.

"When did you learn how to canoe?"

I asked *when*, not *how*, because I didn't want her to think I'd made certain assumptions about her—that her life, her circumstances, wouldn't have contained boats.

"It's new. Alice taught me before she left. She learned at camp."

Stella didn't turn around, so I couldn't see if there was any irony in her expression. If she had some knowingness about my conversational calculations, all the assumptions I made and tried to get out of in my questions.

In the middle of the lake was a small wooded island. Or more like a mound of land thick with trees. Alder trees, for which the lake was once named, though it was actually a pond, according to an old surveyor's map that hung on an office wall up at the lodge. Everyone at camp, though, had always simply called it "the lake." We circled the island and decided not to get out—ticks, and we weren't wearing pants and long sleeves—but we stopped paddling and just floated and Stella told me she had explored the island one day. That if you walked to the middle, there was a clearing, which was spooky because you never saw anybody maintaining it. It was like a crop circle or something.

"Do you believe in that sort of thing?" I asked her. And I

wondered about the clearing—the phenomenon of an absence that just keeps existing, that nature hadn't covered over and restored.

"What, like aliens?"

"The supernatural."

"I'm not sure. I like astrology, though."

"Well, yeah. Your name. It means—"

"Star, yeah. I know." We shared an awkward laugh. Her mother had told her when she was small, I imagined, looking up at the night sky or telling her a story before bed. She'd been told by anyone since then who had tried to hold her attention. She didn't need me to tell her.

"My mother was—is—a huge David Bowie fan. Ziggy Stardust. All that. That's why she named me Stella. Or that's what she's always said."

She turned to face me, smiling, and she didn't ask me what my sign was. She told me. She knew. Or she guessed and she was right. Then she turned back around and we continued floating in the canoe. Silent, aimless, absorbing the sun. A green-and-purple dragonfly landed on my knee and I stared at it, expansively curious, as if I were communing with it, as if its iridescence were going to tell me a secret, as if I were drugged.

We paddled back, eventually, pulled the canoe up onto land and left it there. Stella removed her life jacket and went into the water for a swim, out to the aluminum dock, and I sat in sand that was soft as velour, realizing that I still had my own life jacket belted around me. I finally took it off and leaned back on it. The brightness of the day, filtered through the leaves of a scraggly tree, glowed orange-red through my closed eyelids.

I thought of a hot night when neither of us were sleeping and David and I came down here with flashlights and swam in the dark, warm water.

I thought of Esther and Joe, one September, maybe. After Labor Day, when the season was over but it was still warm, the air still soft but with a hint of something sharper and metallic on the way. The two of them by this lake they'd loved for so long. It wasn't chlorinated, Olympic-sized, it didn't appeal to a new generation of parents or their children.

"We could have built a pool," Esther says.

"We have a goddamn *lake*." Joe's voice cracks as it rises. *A lake! What the fuck is wrong with people?*

To live was to make so many compromises. One had to draw the line somewhere. This was their principled refusal. No pool. And so, the last Alder campers had come and gone more than fifteen years ago. Esther and Joe had considered selling to a developer. Up by the lodge, across the street, there was a housing tract. Homes built in the early '90s that now looked neither new nor old. The people who lived there were what used to pass for upper middle class, better off than many of the people in this town, who inhabited deteriorating houses that had belonged to their grandparents, or boxy, cheaply fabricated homes. I pictured Stella growing up in one of those small, square houses with thin walls, a few towns over. Where her mother told her the meaning of her name.

•

That night I dreamed about the lake, only there were old stone steps that led down to it, the same kind of worn steps that might lead up to an ancient temple. And the lake in the dream was merely an antechamber to a larger body of clear water. I researched the meaning of this, and got so many conflicting interpretations that I decided to hold to the residual feeling that had led me to look it up in the first place: good fortune.

There were two women I knew from New York. We were friends, friendly, though not actively so. They looked alike in the way that white, well-educated, well-dressed women in creative fields can look alike. They were not exactly shy, but they were shrewdly reticent and their shrewd reticence was sometimes mistaken for quietness, softness, by people, men, who weren't as shrewd and smart as they were. About the same age, my age, they both wrote for a middlebrow magazine some people considered highbrow or a highbrow magazine some people considered middlebrow. Depended on the people. I confused these women once in a dream, or one turned into the other, and they'd since become the same person to me. I had to think for a moment when I wanted to distinguish them in my mind. That article about how the fate of an obscure fishery could tell us a lot about climate change. Was that Anna? No, Carrie. Right?

I considered writing quasi-professional emails—of the *I'm still here* variety—to Carrie and Anna. I could write one and send it to both of them.

There was no confusing Stella. She was only herself.

In the athletics shed, Stella and I had found two tennis rackets, strung and in decent shape, the handles not too stripped or eaten away, along with an air-sealed container of tennis balls. Neither of us played tennis, but what a jaunty thing to do. We'd go over to the old courts by the woods, where the sun was never too strong. We'd rig up the crumbling net. We'd have a few matches and then make spritzy drinks. Lying back in Adirondack chairs, admiring our nails.

The only message I'd received that morning was a brief rejection for a position I'd applied to, thinking I might at least be called in for an interview. They'd filled the role internally, I was informed, but they would be happy to keep my materials on file. Best of luck!

So I gathered the tennis equipment and brought it over to Stella's cabin. I knocked on the door, but there was no answer. No note. She'd switched her shift at work, maybe, and I wasn't too concerned. We hadn't made a definite plan. But I had built my day around this. More than my day.

It was as if I were waking up. This was the way dreams ended, without conclusion. It was Friday, I realized. I'd taken out

Stella's splinter on Monday. Days so narcotic that time had slipped from its track. It hadn't even been a week.

When David got home that evening I asked him to go for a walk before dinner, down the road, past the semicircular, flattened spot in the woods that had once been used for archery, and the cabin where the kitchen guys lived in the summer, by the old infirmary. I'd been sick once for what seemed like days in that infirmary. Lying in bed, feverish, in a paneled room with sheer curtains and an old TV, wearing a soft, hot pink T-shirt that said ARUBA on it in white script. I'd never been to Aruba. I don't know where that shirt came from. Aunt Esther was in the room, at one point, with a tray and a deck of well-used playing cards. Navy blue and white on the back, an intricate, scrolling Victorian design. She sat on the bed, placed the tray between us, and taught me how to play hearts. She showed me how to shuffle the pack, bending it into a falling arch. She felt my forehead and held my hand. In and out of sleep: the first time I woke she was still there, the second time I was alone. It didn't occur to me to wonder where my parents were or what was happening to me. I was just there and it was just happening.

I tried to get back to that state—the just being there, the just happening, come what may—as I told David that we had a young woman living in bunk 18 and that I'd gotten to know her a little over the last week. I apologized—I didn't know why I hadn't told him right away. And I didn't, other than I hadn't wanted to fully examine the half-thoughts that surrounded me like the weather. I hadn't wanted to give those thoughts a name, a label that would contain them or that would make them mine, something I had to be responsible for.

"A week?" That was all he said, at first, his voice catching. Then he bent down to the ground, grabbing the end of a large fallen log, and he heaved it out of the path where we were standing. He looked like he wanted twenty more logs to heave, one after the other, even though his hands were already red and marked from gripping the first. He pressed his hands into his hair, elbows in front of his face. There weren't any more logs here and his anger, which rarely flared, had nowhere to go but toward me. "What the *fuck*, Emily."

Just happening wasn't happening, not with my heart beating so fast.

"I don't understand how you just tell me this now like you don't think it's a big deal or that it's disturbing, and *that's* even more disturbing."

"I get that it's a big deal." And I did get it, but not enough to sound convincing.

He pushed the fallen log farther away with his foot, pulled at a low branch; I suppose he still needed something for his hands to do. Despite his strength, David had a gentleness, an agility that made him boyish. He was like a boy, then, with the tree—more athletic than threatening. Still, there was a hole in the ground off to the side of the path, made by a small animal, and part of me wanted to twist away and shrink myself into it, scurry off and disappear. Another part of me, though, felt somewhat indignant. Was it really so terrible, what I'd done? Couldn't I have done much worse?

But then he stopped moving. He sat down on the log and looked up at me. I returned his gaze because I had to, because I didn't want to be a small, scared creature fleeing down a hole. And as he retreated, so did my indignation. He let up, I thought, because his worry outweighed his anger, and because I'd made him worry before. And even if my neurochemistry and my hormones were back in balance, something else was not. I crouched down to meet his level—*okay?*—and he nodded his whole upper body as I shifted to sit beside him.

"I knew something was different, that something was going on with you, but I couldn't figure out what it was," he said. In the absence of antagonism, he reached for information. "What is she like, this squatter?"

I laughed a little, out of some nervous release, finally, and then I fumbled around for adjectives and described her looks, her job, her bike, none of which seemed to impress him as they'd impressed me.

"I mean, she seems nice," I said.

"She *seems* nice? She seems *nice*?" He tried it both ways and neither one satisfied him. "You're the journalist—what do you know about her?"

"You know that's the kind of journalism I was never good at."

"The question-asking kind?"

"I looked her up online. There's not much. Some pictures of her in other people's feeds, at the club where she worked.

It all checks out with what she's told me. I don't know. If she wanted to kill us in our sleep she would have already done it, right?"

"Maybe she wants something else. Something less violent but still, you know, not at all *good*."

We both knew that if I'd really feared she would kill us in our sleep, I would have told him about her immediately, called the authorities, no hesitation. That this was not about that, about my judgment being so questionable. This was about something less obvious, less easy to resolve.

He took in whatever other details I could offer and I thought about an old fight of ours. I no longer remembered the context of it, only that I'd felt accused of something—of wanting too much. And he'd said it wasn't that I wanted too much, it was that I wanted it all for myself. That I could be ungenerous, with him. It shamed me, at the time, because it was true. And I think he was upset with me, there in the woods, not simply because I'd behaved in an off-kilter way that troubled him or because I'd let a stranger into our lives, but because I'd let a stranger into *my* life. I hadn't shared it with him.

"I want to meet her. Let's go over there." He straightened up, keen to move.

"Well, she might not be there. She probably *won't* be there. But if she is, I don't want to, like, ambush her."

"But it's our property." On his feet. "And she's been living here illegally."

I tried to think of a reasonable objection—beyond "So?"— but nothing came.

"Let's just go see if she's even around."

I wouldn't call David impulsive. He doesn't act on whims. But he acts. He is decisive and his decisiveness can be fortifying. Kinetic. Energy moved and something changed. He drew up plans in his mind and executed them in the world, for a living. He made things happen for the both of us. Even moving to this camp was his achievement; I took us to a certain point in the process but he, finally, said yes, and got us here. If he'd said no, we'd have sold the property, we'd still be in Chicago. I certainly wouldn't have left him and come here myself. I wondered, though, if we'd stayed in Chicago, would we still have been together? Would it have been easier to see and to focus on what we didn't have, what we didn't share? Or to think that all we shared was a loss? A generic, almost euphemistic word: *loss*. It papers over a gulf; and the paper holds, surprisingly, for much of the time, so that it makes reorganizing yourself around a disappearance look easy enough, an everyday occurrence, rather than the extraordinary undertaking it is. What did we even lose? Something unknown. We lost potential. But David had said yes, made this relocation happen, kept us together, so that the gulf wasn't between us—it surrounded us, only the two of us—and it was possible, wasn't it, to find new potential within it? And so, despite any inner objections I had there on the path in the woods, we headed over toward Stella's cabin. And as we walked there, those objections began to give way to interest. Something in me wanted to go there with him, not simply to follow him out of a kind of fidelity, but to push it to some new place and see what that pushing would bring.

Stella wasn't there and David went into the bunk to look around. I didn't know if he thought of it as an invasion, and if so, whether that was justified. David, I said, as if to stop him, but without much force, and then I only watched him look around the shadowy place, at the orange crate with a magazine on top of it, the drab green rucksack, a thin hotel towel hanging on a nail, the iron-frame bed Stella had left unmade.

"We just let her live here?" he asked.

"I don't know."

"You're, like, friends with her?"

"Sort of. Yeah."

Weren't we already planning to have all sorts of people staying here? Living, if only for a few days at a time, on our land? We were, essentially, going to host strangers. How far removed from that was this?

They were going to pay us, said David. And he didn't mean this to be greedy or transactional, but in the sense that it necessitated a contract, an understanding between parties, rules.

What were the rules here?

When winter was over, we'd discovered a bird's nest in the eaves of Aunt Esther's house. This after finding one dead baby bird, and then another a few days later, on the brown grass below. David had dug a small, careful hole in the ground. He'd taken a card, easing it under the shriveled creature, carrying it to its grave. Twice. He'd buried each bird in an observant but unceremonial way. We were too old or too expedient to mark the dirt, to recite a prayer or say something whimsical, wistful. And though it reminded me of what we'd hoped for and what we'd grieved, of course, I'd been harder hit at more seemingly random moments: seeing a commercial for debt relief; looking up at light through the glass ceiling panels in the modern wing of the Museum of Fine Arts; finding an old pair of bottle-green sunglasses in one of the kitchen drawers of the house. A clutching in my heart. But when David set about removing or relocating the nest, calling a rescue agency, I thought again: what a good father he would make. I wanted that for him. For us, but especially for him.

I didn't know if Aunt Esther's intention, in leaving me the camp, was to provide us a fresh start. But that's what David turned it into when he said, *yes, let's go.* How he took care of me, took care of us, and how I wanted to be better—more generous—but how I still kept failing him, failing us.

When David was growing up, his family moved around. He spent his very early years in Fort Worth, Texas, then suburban Maryland, and finally northern New Jersey, where his parents still lived. He had attachments to each of these places but none of them was home, exactly. It was like he'd taken extremely extended vacations there. He knew the lay of the land. He had friends. He had memories. Images. A playing field at twilight. A water park. White vinyl chairs in a breakfast nook at a neighbor's house. A boxy forest-green Volvo with a mustard accent stripe. Maroon carpet on the stairs of a movie theater.

The Tudor façade of an apartment house. Tickets on the seat-backs of a New Jersey Transit train. Penn Station.

But because there was an unspoken temporariness to it all, he never really longed to escape where he was, nor did he particularly want to return. These were places he had been and there were other places he would go.

Maybe that's why he wanted to make permanent spaces for people, I had said, offering him my hack analysis when we were getting to know each other. We were in a park in Inwood, where Manhattan reminded me a little of the hilly parts of northern and eastern Paris, the neighborhoods we would wander together a year or two later. Or no, we were on a bench in Brighton Beach, eating *pirozhki*, by the waves of the Atlantic.

He said that was a nice way to look at it. That he didn't have too many illusions about the permanence of the reconfigured bathroom stalls he worked on.

"Well, okay, I can see why you'd maybe feel a little . . . *shitty* about that kind of work," I said.

"Thanks, Dad," he said, and then immediately apologized for calling me Dad. For linking me not with actual fathers, even, but a caricature so associated with puns and bad jokes as to be completely removed from any kind of sexual universe. The apology continued with some more Dad-distancing words I don't remember, then ended with him blurting: "And I do want to have sex with you."

"You do. Want to have sex with me?"

"I do."

"Right here?"

"Is that what you're into?"

We were getting to know each other. We sat on that bench along the boardwalk as if we were rooted to the slats by a rush of intensity, wariness, and—I don't know what else to call it—joy.

The morning after I told David about Stella was Saturday. I woke up late, alone in our bed. David wasn't in the house, but I didn't get anxious. It wasn't unusual. He always told me if he was going down to the lake or somewhere on the edge of camp, but he was probably outside, closer, doing yardwork. He'd made coffee. I poured myself a cup and took it out to the porch. A faint hum of insects. Green everywhere. No humidity or haze but a kind of depth to that green, like a painting done in thick strokes. I stood there barefoot in a loose tank top and underwear, half-dressed in a way I became conscious of only when I heard two voices, from across the road by the lodge. I couldn't make out what they were saying but the tone was friendly and then there was laughter. David and Stella.

The talking stopped and David came around the corner, muttering to himself, repeating part of whatever exchange they had just had, startled a little when he saw me.

Hi, he said.

You've met Stella? I asked.

He'd gone over to her cabin, introduced himself, not sure what to expect really, but she seemed . . . fine? She'd noticed he was holding pruning shears (had he brought them as a prop? as protection?) and asked him if he wanted help. They'd done a little maintenance work together, trimming unwieldy hedges. She was great at it, he said. Like he would have hired her for a summer job and given her a glowing reference.

So, you don't want to call the police or anything, I said.

I had gotten good at reading David over the years, come to know his body, and the expression on his face seemed to say: *No, you can keep her.* It also betrayed embarrassment. Maybe at the way he'd reacted the day before when I'd told him about Stella? Maybe at the way he'd stepped into my place with Stella just now? Both, possibly. He set the shears on a worn wicker chair, moved up behind me, and put his hand through the arm opening of my top. He put his other hand down my underwear. I spilled the coffee. *Not out here.* I pushed him inside the house, pulled him toward me, slipping on the rug in the hall, down to the floor.

We knew each other's body so well and still—or maybe therefore—they gave us away. His head between my legs was all that mattered, and then, coming back to myself, to him, I exchanged the favor, but it wasn't a favor and it wasn't an exchange this time, not an even one. I didn't exactly surrender something, he didn't exactly take anything from me, but something was transferred from me to him so that, after, I felt at a loss. I'd had something, some source of desire, that was mine alone, and now I had shared it with him, and I wasn't sure if sharing it with him was an act of generosity or one of betrayal.

The next time I saw Stella I couldn't look her in the eye.

THE STORM

One summer when I was a camper at Alder, they had evacuated us to the regional high school in advance of a hurricane. Like all the other children at the camp, I was instructed to take my sleeping bag, my pillow, and a change of clothes. Though the building must have had windows, in my memory we didn't see daylight for two days. It was strange being in a school we'd never attend, devoid of people we'd never know. Trophy displays and long rows of lockers, painted cinder-block walls. We hadn't spoken to our parents before we left. We packed up and followed orders. Two days, it seemed, spent in a gigantic bunker or a spacecraft.

The latest weather forecasts David and I had heard this week hadn't warned of anything as potentially destructive as that long-ago storm. We didn't need to evacuate. But we were cautioned about high winds, downed branches, power outages, flooding. We bought groceries and tested the generator. David decided not to go to work.

It was our duty, wasn't it, to check on Stella? To invite her, but really insist, that she come up to the house, for her own safety, because this was going to be more than a soaking summer rain.

When the trees began to shiver and the temperature dipped, I pulled on a jacket and went to her cabin. The impersonal urgency of the situation—dangerous weather beyond our control—tempered my hesitancy. Hesitancy that she would think I had an ulterior motive, hesitancy that I did. But I was able to look her in the eye again and she seemed happy to see me, grateful that I'd offered her the option. She'd been thinking of asking if she could stay with us for the worst of it. She had on a hip-length, striped mohair sweater, and through it I could see a T-shirt from a high school sports team. Sometimes I thought I wanted her clothes, and other times I realized I would have to be her in order to wear them.

She slipped her phone into the pocket of her jeans, got her backpack together quickly, and, on our way to the house, she kept her hands tucked into the long cuffs of her sweater. I felt a little like I was walking her to her first day at a new school. And then, too, like she was walking me to mine. A kind of excitement and trepidation that seemed out of proportion to the action of heading up the front stairs of the house, opening the door for her, but then, what would have been in proportion? I didn't know.

I had, that first afternoon that we met, removed her splinter, come home, and instinctively, almost unthinkingly, gone through the rooms of this house wondering how she would see them. How, by extension, she would see me. She was everywhere, in every room, when I'd imagined it. Now that she was really here, though, standing in the hall, her hands stuck safe in her sweater cuffs, she was still alert, still ascertaining, but she didn't stride in, did not make herself perfectly comfortable. She was waiting for me to set the tone and I had frozen, for a moment, before a kind of practiced hospitality kicked in. *Oh, come on in! Here, let's put your bag down.* I regretted that I hadn't asked her in before this, or at least not beyond the front porch. I hadn't wanted to seem too forward. Which is really just to say, I think, that I hadn't wanted to be rejected by her.

In the living room, where the windows were still open, the curtains billowed in before getting sucked back against the screens. Stella looked around, down at the patterns of the rugs, up at all the books on the shelves and in piles against a wall, interested but a little helpless, like she was looking at a façade of hieroglyphics. I didn't want to point to any particular book, introduce it to her as a favorite in some way that would probably come off as condescending. I didn't understand why this was so difficult, here, now, when it had been so easy with her, by the lake, in her bunk.

Because of David in the house? But it was David who saved us. *Hey.* Coming in casually. *Hey, Stella.* Trimming weeds together had bonded them, had it? Made them comrades in yardwork, given them a basis to be relaxed around each other. *Hey, David.* She turned from the books. *Thanks for taking me in.* He motioned: *It's nothing. What are you even talking about? Of course.*

We settled in. We lit candles on the table as it darkened outside. Made grilled cheese on good bread and tomato soup with basil leaves. Opened a bottle of red wine. We didn't lose electricity but we played board games and worked jigsaw puzzles as if we had.

At one point, David and Stella were in the kitchen, baking brownies, while I lay on the couch and listened as they talked loudly about ex-girlfriends.

"Alice, God, she sounds like a type," said David. As was his girlfriend in college, Lauren. "Strong opinions, not much doubt or humility."

"She has so many opinions and she feels pretty strongly about all of them," said Stella.

"It's kind of great, at first," said David. "But exhausting, eventually."

"And then what?" asked Stella.

Then, years later, David theorized, this type would befriend you on social media, expecting you to like all their many, strongly opinionated posts.

"Was Alice cheap?" David asked, as if confirming that this quality was part of the profile.

"Yeah, kind of. Like she expected me to get her free drinks and stuff when I was working, even though she could more than afford it."

"With Lauren, she never had her wallet, or she never had money on her, even though she had more money than I did. I ended up paying for everything. It was always little things, but it added up, not just in terms of money. It was selfishness, a lack of reciprocity, of generosity."

I'd heard enough about Lauren, mostly when David and I were getting to know each other, to feel that she maintained no hold on him. He didn't secretly long for her. There was no one I secretly longed for anymore, either. There were people I thought about from time to time, but what I longed for had become free-floating, objectless. Until I met Stella, that is. And it's not that she became the object of my desire. Not exactly. More like she reminded me that longing could sometimes, for an instant, here and there, be met.

David and Stella joined me while the brownies were in the oven, David scooting himself in next to me on the couch so my head rested on his leg. Stella looked through our records and turned on the stereo. Not party music. Moody, lush, minor-key songs. And even though David and I were in a position to be watching her, as she hummed and read liner notes, it seemed to me that she and David, as they had been in the kitchen, were the pair. They reminded me of the men in Cassavetes's *Husbands*. Their camaraderie. David and Stella had developed an attachment—or, at any rate, I wanted them to have an attachment, wanted to see them that way—like those married, middle-class, middle-aged male friends, with all their roiling feelings, who, in the wake of losing one of their own, get drunk in 1969 New York and then go off carousing to London. I was the suburban wife you briefly glimpse. If all this made me a little jealous, it was outweighed by relief. I sank deeper into the cushions of the couch.

David asked her the question I never had: Why this place? How did she and Alice even know about the camp? And I wondered why it hadn't occurred to me to ask. She'd shown up and that was all that had mattered to me.

Stella was happy to tell him. Her mother, a nurse, had worked in the infirmary over the course of two summers. It would have been long after I was a camper and just before Esther and Joe closed the place. From what Stella could tell, her mother liked the job, the staff, the girls she took care of. There'd been a day when Stella, for reasons she couldn't remember or was never quite aware of—she would have been five or six—had come to work with her mother. She'd sat in a folding aluminum chair while a dozen or so girls lined up through the infirmary door to receive their morning medications. She'd watched TV, the same black-and-white set I'd probably watched when I was sick there. A counselor took her to the arts-and-crafts building where she'd made a mask out of glitter and glue. Later she'd gone down to the lake and put her toes in the water with an older girl who, she recalled, had looked like Anne Frank.

"Is that terrible? Is that like saying all Jewish girls look the same to me? Like Anne Frank?"

"I don't know," said David. "Emily used to kind of look like Anne Frank."

"I have her coloring," I said. "It's Jewish. Eastern European."

I was slightly offended by David's observation but I wasn't sure why.

"You have her eyes," said Stella. "I was obsessed with Anne Frank for a while."

"You were?" I asked.

"Yeah. We learned about her for like one day in school but I kept going. I read everything. I wanted to visit Amsterdam to see the Anne Frank House. If anyone asked me where in the world I wanted to go, I would say Amsterdam for that reason. Not like I got that question a lot. But, you know. I don't know why I was *so* interested in her. Maybe, in a weird way, because she reminded me of the girl who took me to the lake, and that was always one of those memories for me that was hazy but also really strongly stamped."

"There are yearbooks in the lodge, from each summer at Alder. We could look through them and you could probably find out who the girl was," I said.

David tried not to smile and Stella lowered her gaze. I got the joke a beat late. That all the girls in the yearbooks would look the same to her, like Anne Frank. And neither David nor Stella seemed to have the urge, as I instinctively did, to identify or know anything more about that particular girl.

"Have you ever been to Amsterdam?" I asked.

"I haven't left the country. Well, Canada once."

I realized what it was about her that was unusual: For someone who hadn't traveled very much or very far, she was one of the least provincial people I'd ever met. It wasn't that she had no attachments. It was that her attachments didn't seem to narrow her life, they seemed to make her want more life. If she wasn't worldly, it was only because she hadn't yet had the opportunity; she already had the outlook. This place, all the girls with Anne Frank eyes, had lodged itself in her, a place she didn't belong to but which belonged to her.

The context of the conversation she'd had early on with Alice about the camp was lost to Stella now—what remained were voices, sun through a window, squaring itself on Alice's bed—but Alice had said they should go back and see what it was like now. Alice had left, Stella had stayed.

The oven timer dinged and I went for the brownies, as the rain battered the windows, the side of the house, the roof. So much of it, as if a large lake had been turned upside down over us, repeatedly. Not a refreshing rain, a mud-making one. But we were safe in here. Still drinking our wine. I couldn't tell what time of day it was. Clocks no longer mattered.

David and Stella, I could hear from the hall, were those men in the movie again, the fulsome husbands, sitting in the back room of the kind of New York bar that no longer exists, windowless, all dark wood and desaturated colors, with strange old patrons dressed in synthetic fabrics and cheap knits, singing, badly, songs I didn't know. The air between David and Stella wasn't pressurized. There seemed to be no subtext when they talked. He asked her questions about her life and she answered: Her mother still worked as a nurse but in the western part of the state and had a boyfriend Stella wasn't crazy about. She had one older sister who lived in the Pacific Northwest. Her dad had been out of the picture for a long time.

"Does your mom know you're here?" my husband asked.

"No, actually. She probably thinks I'm still at my sublet room in the city."

From the hallway arch, in the low light, they were a slow-shutter photograph: Stella with flecks of mascara in her eyelashes, her mouth turned up at the corners. David's long fingers under his chin. I entered the room and I liked the three of us together. I liked that Stella wasn't mine alone.

We stayed that way, talking, not talking, until the worst of the storm had passed, it seemed, but there was no question that Stella would spend the night here.

She followed me upstairs when I went to get her clean sheets for the extra bedroom and she accepted my offer of a T-shirt to wear as pajamas. The extra room was one we'd left as we'd found, with its wallpaper full of floral sprigs, a room that still belonged to Esther and Joe. But first I stepped into my room, the one I shared with David, and as I opened my dresser drawer, I could see out of the corner of my eye that Stella had followed me in from the doorway, training her gaze on my nightstand. So I looked there, too, at the pair of black sunglasses, a stack of books, an orange plastic pill bottle, elastic hair bands, a glass tumbler half-full of water. None of it was especially revealing, not even the antidepressants. She didn't know I still had the note she wrote on blue scrap paper, kept safe in the drawer. But I did still have it, and now our eyes met for a moment and it was as if we'd accidentally touched hands then pulled quickly away and then I didn't know where to look, what to say.

To break some tension, perhaps, she did a weird little dance with her arms, part mime, part tai chi.

"Gimme my shirt, lady," she said.

"Sweet dreams," I said.

Her self-possession fascinated me. Not because it was total and unfailing but because it faltered and then rebounded. There was a flexibility, an elasticity to it. I was never so self-possessed as Stella at twenty-two. I'm still not. So often in a situation my first question is: *Am I doing something wrong?* I care less and less what the answer is, but that's still the first question.

The storm blew on through the night, gone by morning, leaving our house mostly fine, it seemed. Sun through the seam in the curtains when I woke up next to David, rolled into him, my head on the side of his chest. Half-asleep, he held my arm. I imagined Stella might be gone, might have left before dawn. Left the T-shirt I gave her folded on the guest bed.

She wasn't in her room but I found her down in the kitchen, wearing, over the T-shirt, a silk robe, navy blue with peach blooms. There was something florid and decadent, something—I want to say moneyed—about her in that robe.

"This was in the closet. I hope you don't mind."

"No. It's beautiful. It must have belonged to my aunt." It was strange, that robe, of a piece with what I had thought was the singular, anomalous glamour of the upstairs bathroom, all glossy, dark green tiles, half the wall papered in white with a pattern of black abstract line drawings, an elegant faucet for the porcelain sink. Esther's doing, no doubt, but was the bathroom intended as a start to an unfinished thought or was it always meant to be contained, of itself?

How had I never noticed the robe there? How was it not too musty, the fabric not too degraded to wear?

"Smells a little mothbally, but."

"You should keep it. You should wear it all the time."

I didn't quite realize I'd said that last part out loud, but she laughed, so I did too.

"Thanks for letting me stay here."

"Of course. Thanks for making coffee."

"I'm good at it," she said, so matter of fact I couldn't detect any sarcasm or pride on her part.

I opened windows, a freshness filtering in from outside, but when David came down it wasn't like the day and night before. All that chumminess, their ease and mine, had been replaced by a quiet fatigue, like the end of a long drive in a car. He seemed a little worn out. And a little wary. I didn't remember what I'd dreamed about, but I wondered if David did somehow, if my dream was suffusing his waking hour, and if Stella figured into it.

Out on the porch, where we took our coffee, branches and debris had been blown about, landing in the small field in front of the house where you could just make out the old contours of a baseball diamond. It was Saturday, and David and I had the day ahead to ourselves, no plans except for cleaning up whatever mess the storm had caused. But Stella said she needed to get moving, if she was going to be on time for her shift.

She started to take off the robe and, though she had clothes on underneath, the gesture was unnerving. As if she were stripping for us.

"Oh no. You really should keep that," I said.

And it was all I could do not to dash inside, find a blanket, and throw it over her, to end the scene, get her off the stage, out of the situation. Get us out of it. But which us? David was in the doorway, drinking his coffee, watching me fix the robe back on Stella, snugly tying the sash. Or perhaps he was only watching Stella accepting my adjustments. I couldn't be sure which.

"I'll walk back with you to the bunk," I offered. "See if there's any damage."

"Sure. Okay."

She wore the black high-top canvas sneakers she always did, and I wore the expensive rubber boots that covered my calves—what I bought, when we moved here, as "country attire." But I was wrong to want them, they were an extravagance, an affectation, and I wanted to give them to Stella. Take the robe, take these boots, take it all. I'm not sure what I even meant by "all." And I didn't say any of this. We walked in silence until she told me how much she liked David. That usually when she spent much time with someone's husband, or boyfriend more frequently, given her age, she didn't get it. What was she doing with him? How did it work, when he was so . . . nowhere near her?

"You were prepared to think less of me?" My laugh rang out into the small meadow we mucked through. "For my choice in husband? Or for, what, even having a husband?"

Stella didn't reply right away, but looked at me, a little taken aback, even slightly hurt, as though trying to gauge if I were upset with her.

"I just . . . I meant it as a good thing," she said. "Like, something to aspire to. I can see it, that's all."

Before I could ask what it was that she could see, we'd reached the bunk. She ran inside for her red polo uniform and her bike, which she must have stowed for the storm. She squished it through the muddy grass a little, onto a solid path, and then she was gone, and I was perplexed. What had I wanted her to say? She'd liked David. It was a good thing. We were aspirational, even? Why should a comment like this have left me, standing there on the wet, open ground, with the sense of being safely categorized by Stella and put away. Of being considered done with. Of being on the outside and wanting back in.

To push the thought down, I surveyed the scene. The reason, after all, that I'd come this way. One of the shutters had come loose and hung off its hinges. Aside from that, everything seemed all right. There were probably plenty of other places, structures, things for me and David to assess on the property in the wake of the storm, but instead of going directly back to the house, I went to the lodge and headed to the room where all the old yearbooks were shelved. An archive of sorts, though looking through their pages wasn't so much going back in time as visiting a parallel world where the same systems were in place but their orchestration was different, where something you'd always known by one name was here known by another, you recognized the words but they had different meanings. I was there, in those pages, as a girl. Anne Frank in dark athletic shorts with light piping and a T-shirt that said ARUBA on it in white script. You know who else was there? I found her, the assistant nurse who worked those last couple of summers. Everybody in those black-and-white staff photos was identified in the accompanying captions, including Robin Dart, the squinting, smiling woman in a printed scrub top who looked exactly like a slightly older version of her daughter. Stella.

I didn't know how long I'd been here. Long enough for David to come looking and discover me sitting among decades of spiral-bound yearbooks splayed out over the linoleum floor.

"Whoa," he said. He looked almost impressed by the methodical disarray.

"Hi," I said, a little embarrassed, but grateful to be found.

HOUSECOATS

Leaving Chicago, we'd taken a busy four-lane road into a suburb with low-slung warehouses and corporate buildings broken up by a couple of uncharming churches, and old developments of small dun-colored houses and apartments with synthetic siding made to resemble stone. I didn't know what this had looked like in the fifties or early sixties, when it was built. New? Nice? Or was it always—forever—down at the heels?

David was at the wheel of our Honda and I was looking out, beginning to settle into a meditative gaze, when I saw, in one of these street-side apartments, a figure standing in a picture window, her hands pressed to the glass. I thought she was a girl at first, but she was an old woman, white, wearing a hot-pink house dress, platinum hair set in curlers, garish lipstick. She seemed like a hallucination—David clearly hadn't seen her—and then she seemed to me more like a painting, or a photograph. No longer a person but an image hung on a wall or printed in an art book. I wanted to stare at her as much as I wanted to turn away. And it was only a glimpse I'd caught anyway as we drove on. But I couldn't shake a feeling, an association. That she was encroaching on me even as she receded. I had only wanted to look at her for longer because I knew I was only looking. Those were the terms.

I remembered a woman like this from my childhood. These women used to exist outside of Boston, too, but I hadn't seen anyone like them here for years and certainly not since we'd moved back. The kind of women who wore housecoats. In the late '70s and early '80s, traces of the '50s and '60s remained—not yet vintage, only dated. I suspected Robin Dart, no more than a dozen years older than me, knew the kind of women I meant, knew them better even than I did, and rescued herself from their fate through her love for David Bowie and a nursing degree. My memory is a fragment, a few frames from a film. I'm very young with my father in a house with pink walls, pink carpet, a thin white iron railing inside, a sort of banister that extends to become a barrier between two zones of carpet. Porcelain plates on part of the wall as decoration. We'd walked up concrete steps to ring the bell. We're there to drop something off, a professional holiday gift, a bottle of liquor. It's cheery. She's older and her husband is there. He's short and round and balding, in belted trousers and a too-snug plaid shirt. Maybe it's the string of lights along the wall and in the window, foggy with condensation, the gift of liquor, but I have some sense that these people are not like us. We're not like them. It's very dim, it's feeling along the wall in a dark space, but it's there, this comprehension of difference. My father is giving them a gift for Christmas, a holiday we don't celebrate. The difference is that they're not Jewish and we are, and this may be the first time I come to be aware that "Jewish" is a whole universe of codes and signs I will learn to read.

I've asked my father about this moment and he has no memory of it, who these people were, why we might have been there.

THE INTERVIEW

The town we lived in was the kind of place that a certain demographic—old enough to know that a swath of popular culture no longer speaks to them, but not so old as to stop identifying as "youngish"; city-oriented and with some spare time and income to spend on restaurants, occasional travel, books and music, clothes—might go to get away for a few days. They might have stayed at our resort, had we been able to pull it off.

I was part of that demographic. Or thought I was. But I was also here all the time. This place wasn't an escape for me. Let's go to Boston, I'd say to David. A city I'd only known as a child, familiar but also foreign. The scale of it, the social tone.

We had a few friends there, David had colleagues he'd fallen in with easily enough, but I felt I almost had to learn a new language in order to understand people I came in contact with, for the interactions to come off. I was too friendly or not friendly enough.

New York I had always and immediately understood: direct but chatty. There was a warmheartedness to it, a pulse. You could find this in other cities but never in such a pure form. It was always diluted, by laidback disinterest, bored complacency, or the judgmental reserve insecurity creates. We'd go to Boston, to see a movie or go out to dinner, and it wasn't a question of my clothes being too high end or too low, it was that, regardless, I'd be dressed in a way that looked like I put too much thought into how I dressed. I didn't know what to wear or how to think about clothes anymore. If I really spun it out, I didn't know how to think about thought anymore.

All of this became amplified when I got a call about a job interview, the prospect of which had started to seem so hypothetical as to be unreal. Like receiving an invitation to a royal ball. I knew I couldn't just walk around camp all day forever. That sooner rather than later, if I didn't start contributing, we would have to sell the property. I knew that, but it had reached the point where I was sending out résumés mostly so I could tell David I'd been sending out résumés, so he wouldn't be upset with me. If I expected to feel anything about hearing back from a potential employer, I'd thought it would have been relief, at having good news for David. I hadn't expected to feel excited, to feel possibility, for myself.

I brought Stella inside—*you're not done with me, not yet*—led her upstairs, and opened my closet. Maybe because we had a goal in mind, a purpose that delivered us from ourselves, the exposure, the tension I had felt when she'd been in my room that night of the storm had slackened. Even as I stood there in my bra and underwear, putting on clothes and taking them off as she watched. Or maybe because of it. There was still a charge, but it had become bearable, manageable. I could direct it in a useful way.

Try this, she said. *Okay, how about this? Oh, this! Yeah, that's it. You look so fucking good!* Pleased with herself, pleased with me.

She'd picked out a pair of cropped trousers and a slouchy silk top for an effect that was loose but not entirely without edge. We decided I should look like I had put just enough effort in to look effortless. I would be meeting with Samira, a woman who'd started an online retail venture of clothing and home goods that were ethically and sustainably produced but also met a certain fashion standard. Her small company was faring well enough to need another person to handle its communications needs. From what I could tell after looking her up, we were around the same age. Our eyes originated from the same part of the world, long, long ago; hers weren't Anne Frank–like, exactly, but they were Semitic, deep-set with dark shadows. She'd grown up the child of diplomats—her father was from Spain, her mother was Lebanese—she was born in the United States and then they'd spent a stretch in Turkey and then a longer one in Canada. Before ending up in Boston, a move that I gathered had something to do with her academic husband, Samira had worked internationally as an editorial stylist.

All of which raised the critical question: Which shoes to

wear? We tried it with flats (if Samira were short) and with heels (if she were tall). I couldn't determine her height from photos.

"How does she sound?" Stella asked.

"Can you tell someone's stature by their voice?"

"I usually get a vibe off the way someone talks."

I asked if I could take her with me to the interview. She could collect vibes in the lobby and transmit them to me. "Be my guru," I said. "We'll get this job together."

She shook her head, not like I was being silly, but like her powers unfortunately didn't work that way.

I didn't necessarily believe in her powers, but I believed in *her*. Stella had told me she didn't want to be a barista forever and I believed that she wouldn't be. But I hadn't asked what she did want and how she envisioned getting there. I wasn't sure how to ask without sounding judgmental or oblivious. I had been raised with advantages she didn't have, and still, look where I was. But then, I wasn't Stella. Stella wasn't me.

In my last year of college, at the university career center, I had searched an alumni database that provided me contact information for an editor at a downtown weekly in New York. I was nervous on the phone but he was enthusiastic, happy to talk and tell me about his work, putting me at ease. Ideally, he asked, what do you want to write? Ideally, I told him, I'd like to write about film. He didn't burst out in derisive laughter. He just said, *Yeah.* Yeah: *get in line, join the club.* I got in line. That paper was gone now. And even films, it seemed, didn't really exist as such anymore.

The day of the interview, I drove into the city without getting into an accident, located parking in a garage, took in my reflection in a storefront window, and nodded, pleased. I did all of this, like a fully functioning adult. It had occurred to me that I had stopped considering myself an adult, that it happened sometime after I was about to become a parent and then didn't. That moving to Alder, which I had thought of as a little daring but was mostly level-headed, only compounded the regression.

But here I was, a grown woman, who understood the value of time and presentation. I'd arrived early because I didn't know the neighborhood all that well. Fort Point. An old manufacturing district along a channel that led to the harbor, transformed in recent years. David and I once had dinner at a nearby restaurant where we had to reserve a table weeks in advance. The area had been an enclave of industrial buildings from the nineteenth and early twentieth centuries, David said then. And though I'd already known that much, I hadn't known the architectural terms he'd used—classical revival, Romanesque. Masonry and timber construction. I hadn't known that iron, sugar, and wool had once come through the wharves. That you could, if you wanted, trace whole histories of wealth and exploitation, through these streets. And it struck me now, walking slowly on this cloudless day, calming my pre-interview nerves, that the few other associations I had with this part of town concerned work.

The first was a memory from around the time my father and I dropped the holiday liquor off with the older couple in

the pink room. It's winter and it must be school vacation because I'm at a childcare program while my parents work. I've
spent a lot of my life here, it's a familiar place, a repurposed
Victorian house in our town outside Boston, and I know all
the teachers. Suzanne, with her long dark hair, her high-waist
jeans and ski sweaters, is my favorite. They've planned a special
field trip for us, into the city, to the Children's Museum right
around here in Fort Point, but that's not what I remember.
Before we go to the museum, we go to Suzanne's apartment,
which is only a few blocks away. She sits us all down in a circle
and we eat our packed lunches in a cavernous room on wide,
scuffed-up floorboards painted black. The walls are brick and a
huge, arched window opens onto gray sky. There's an unmade
bed in the corner illuminated by a lamp, a few empty wooden
frames leaning against a wall, and a long curtain that separates
this area from a room she calls her studio. At the time, the
details don't conform into an interpretation—that the large
wooden pieces are stretcher bars for canvas, that Suzanne is
an artist who lives in a loft and takes care of kids to pay her
rent. I only know that she lives in a kind of space I've never
seen before. That my parents don't live in a place like this and I
somehow know they never will. They're not like Suzanne. And
I want to be like her, not them.

The second memory was newer but even so, it was already
a long time ago. I've finished my sophomore year of college,
I'm home for a few months, and in addition to a summer job, I
have an unpaid internship two days a week at a foundation for
filmmakers. They award grants and loan equipment out but

they have no money—this isn't Hollywood or New York. I can attend screenings and other events for free, though, and I'm getting experience, as they say. In an office of three rooms with worn industrial carpeting and a configuration of whatever furniture was left by former tenants, I mostly answer calls on a relatively new phone system, the most up-to-date device in the room. I'm nervous when I first learn how to hold, transfer, and otherwise direct calls because I don't want to get it wrong and because Nick is standing over me, showing me which buttons to press. I'm jumpy around him, but something sinuous and slow is also taking place. Nick does many things—works here, teaches at the art college, mostly wears black, makes me nervous. He's not yet thirty years old. One day he shows up in a white T-shirt because it's too hot out for black. There's a task that needs doing, he tells me. It's taking a sack of mail, about three feet high, to the post office by South Station. I'm not sure why it has to go to that specific post office, but it does, and before 2:30 p.m. It's a trip on the T far enough away to require a transfer between lines. We can't pay for cab fare, he says, but we'll do it together. It'll be fun. He doesn't have to go with me, so he must *want* to go with me, I think. And I spend most of the morning thinking this, thinking about him while filing and doing mailing-list data entry. He's late getting back from lunch, though, and this is before everyone has cell phones. There's no way to reach him and this mail has to go out, so I do it myself, struggling to find a good way to hold the heavy, unwieldy sack. There's no good way. People in the street and on the train give me sorry looks but nobody moves to help.

I want to drag the bag but I'm too conscientious to do that. The postal worker I finally reach at the bulk mail area is like a long-lost relative, and in the few seconds where he relieves me of my burden, it's a homecoming.

"Godspeed," he says to the sack, heaving it into a cart.

Once it's out of my hands, I've never been so light, so weightless, I might float away on the breeze by the water, the channel, which cools me off and keeps me from immediately feeling disgusting. The disgust comes, though, increasingly, on the subway platform, and when I climb the stairs back to the office, I'm damp with sweat but it's not in any way sexy. It's made my hair frizz in a way I don't like and I smell. Nick looks at me like I've fallen off a treadmill, like it's painful to watch but hard not to laugh.

"Oh, fuck. I'm sorry," he says. "I got caught up and totally forgot." He doesn't say with what. "I'm really sorry."

"I feel gross," I say. "It's so fucking hot out." I should be filled with hate and anger toward him but it's not there. Anything that sharp and solid has melted from me. Only abjection remains.

He gets me water from the tap in one of the random mugs by the mini-fridge and I gulp it down. And then he does something that almost makes me cry. He asks if I want an extra T-shirt of his he's left at his desk.

In the bathroom, where the stall is thickly painted black, the fluorescent light is falling down, and duct tape holds white tiles to the wall, I wash myself at the sink and I don't put my bra back on before putting on his shirt. It's cool against my skin, it's clean but it has his scent and I want to live in it. I see in the mirror that wearing his shirt somehow makes my hair look better, mussed up. I could make this my style, make it work for me.

He's back by his desk in the other room when I come out and I'm grateful there's no admiring glance, no patting himself on the back for doing me this favor. I start on some clerical work, moving my tongue to my upper lip, tasting salt from sweat that had dried there and not been washed off. I wait for the phones to ring and I don't see him again until the end of the day. When his girlfriend, I assume, shows up to meet him. Dark sunglasses pushed up into her sooty hair, smudgy eyeliner, a black dress that is essentially a very long tank top. Maybe she's not his girlfriend—not to the extent that she knows I'm wearing his shirt. Or maybe she's just pretending not to know or care. But Nick pauses, pulls back a little, when he enters the room and looks at me in his shirt, not with self-satisfaction or pity but something else. Some new interest that hasn't fully formed into desire. While this is happening, she is talking, from somewhere in the muffled distance, about it being too sticky to sit outside and drink and so they should go to the air-conditioned repertory theater with the Fassbinder retrospective.

"Have a good weekend, Emily." He looks back, twice. Figuring something out.

Nothing ever happened between us, I would say whenever the topic of old crushes came up in conversation with friends, and with David once. But a whole world opened up in a look.

I used to sleep in his T-shirt. I have no idea where it is now but I kept it for years.

A discreet sign marked the entrance to the building where Samira worked, a three-story brick warehouse with tall windows, converted to retain the dust-beam shadowiness of the original. The ground floor was a lofty, empty space—mostly an open stairwell of iron and concrete whose proportions seemed designed to slightly, pleasantly displace you. To make you feel you were in transition, on your way to someplace you wanted to be.

I switched my flats for the heels and headed up two flights to the top. I pressed a button, heard a click, and pushed a metal door into what looked more like an inviting living room than an office. There were large plants. Polished wood. A pair of lamps with malachite bases. An atmosphere of warm luxuriousness that I understood to be a reflection or extension of Samira.

Before I was introduced to her, I met with Jenna, tiny as an actress, coiled into a black sweatshirt in the cold air-conditioning. Pretty, symmetrical face, light eyes that landed on you, flitted away, came back. I towered over her, but like an elk that would saunter off if it lost interest. Astonishingly, she did her best to welcome and hold me there. Advantage: me. She struck me as competent and resourceful, but the roomy sweatshirt made her seem not intimidatingly so. She didn't tell me exactly what her role was but she seemed to have most of the responsibilities of an assistant as well as some of the authority of a second-in-command and the relied-upon judgment of a gatekeeper. I passed, evidently, and she let me through to see Samira, who told me to call her Sam when she came by to take me to a different corner of the space, set off by glass partitions.

Sam was around my size, dressed in vintage Levi's, a gray T-shirt, a navy blazer. She didn't look me up and down, not obviously, but she seemed to take me in, to scan me with an extrasensory power. I wondered if she understood that I'd put just enough effort in to look effortless today, and if so, would this recognition interest her? Would she sense her own kind?

"Hi," she said then, as we sat, after we'd already said hello, as if this were our real language and now we could freely speak it. There was a warmth, a luxuriousness to her tone, and as we freely spoke our language, it wasn't simply old professional habits kicking in—the ability to talk to people. It was a re-freshment, a reawakening—interwoven with the discussion of my work history, establishing that what she needed was some-thing I could offer, was the kind of expressive, giving conver-sation that returns to you some part of yourself. When it took a personal turn, it only felt natural.

"I really didn't know what to make of this city for a long time," she said, after detailing the path that had brought her here. "And I didn't know what to make of myself in it."

"When we moved here I thought I had forgotten how to think," I said.

"Yes! I would go to these faculty parties with Olivier, my

husband—*parties* is too generous a word—but I would go and stand there, glass of wine in hand, early evening in a richly paneled room, leaded windows, ivy just outside, the kind of environment I might have once styled for a shoot, and the women would ignore me and the men would compliment me but always on the wrong thing, in the wrong way. Or I'd listen to them, the women and the men, tell me all about their work and never once ask me about what I did or what I thought. It was this total excess of self-regard combined with—"

"A complete lack of curiosity?"

She nodded in exaggerated affirmation.

"Like they knew only what they knew and that was all there was to know?" I added.

"And they don't know how to read your signals and you start to forget that anyone does."

My eyes were drawn to the shelves of art and fashion books along the wall. Volume upon volume of signals.

"It really fucks you up!" She laughed. "I think it's fair to say I started this whole project out of spite. But it's grown, of course. *I've grown*." Her smile-frown scorned the whole enter-prise of self-betterment, of personal growth, but then undercut that with a hint of earnestness. "I mean, I wouldn't want you to get the wrong idea."

"But those are the best kind of ideas," I said.

It was a conversation that reminds you that you can still carry on a conversation, that under the right circumstances it can come back to you just like that, and that just maybe, occa-sionally, the purpose of life is enjoyment. I want to describe the experience with Samira like colored dye injected into water, the moment when it's swirling, creating trails.

It stunned me a bit, after. We'll be in touch soon, she'd said, clasping my hand, transferring some promise for the future. On the stairs, on my way out, I kept returning to that moment. And on the sidewalk, swapping out my shoes, and crossing the street that led out to Fort Point Channel to walk along the waterway, I thought: *I want to do this. With Samira.* What was this feeling? The desire to keep walking, to stay in this world I had entered.

Like a well-heeled tourist, I wandered for a while, stopping in a sleek, airy café, to order an Arnold Palmer. I didn't have a city anymore, but maybe I could make this one mine again.

I thought about calling David, getting on the T, going by his office, but I didn't. I considered texting Stella, because we were in each other's contacts now, but I didn't do that either. I just finished my drink and continued to walk, past the landmarked architecture, looking up at arched windows and wondering which one Suzanne the artist lived behind in another life. Eventually, I made it back to the garage, to the car. I hardly remembered driving home.

THE DINNER PARTY

I wanted the evening to be celebratory. There was no occasion to mark, no news to cheer, but I had this feeling, this compressed fizziness, a sense of being on a cusp. I tried to keep it to myself but it leaked out here and there. I caught myself whistling themes from old sitcoms no longer in syndication. Doing little dances around David. Sliding my feet, making geometric motions with my arms. A celebration of cusps, then. It was Saturday, four days after my interview with Samira, who'd responded quickly and warmly to the thank-you email I'd sent. *More soon*, she'd written.

Late afternoon light. Stella and David were out on the back porch, setting the table. I was in the kitchen, music playing while I made a salad, when I heard Liz and Felix drive over the gravel outside. Old friends. We'd known each other for so long I sometimes had to stop and think of the origins—that I knew Liz from our very first year of college, then she met Felix, then I met David. We all lived in New York for a time, then we moved, then they moved, and now here we were in proximity to each other again.

I headed out front. *So good to see you!* we all seemed to say at once, and it was really true. In the months since we'd lived at Alder, we'd been to their house and met them out once or twice, but this was the first time we'd had them over. We weren't the closest friends anymore, we didn't confide in each other that much. But I knew I *could* confide, in Liz especially, and it was this level of trust, I thought, mingled with a sense of possibility, that made being around them comfortable without ever being boring.

"Emily, this place!"

Liz stretched her arms overhead and out as far as they would go. She had a strong body, lean but graceful, that motherhood hadn't taken. Liz was a choreographer. Though she hadn't done so much choreography lately, which I gathered was something of a sore spot, and now I remembered how a mutual friend had once posted about successfully registering her children for various intricately timed summer activities, and had used the word *choreography* to describe the accomplishment. Liz took a screenshot and texted me: "That is not fucking choreography!! That's called scheduling. Get the fuck over yourself." I liked how fiercely Liz valued her work. That, and how exquisitely petty she could be.

Liz and Felix had two children, a four- and a six-year-old, whom they'd left with a sitter. We'd promised to have their whole family out here but Liz insisted on limiting it to the adults this evening. She was giddy and liberated to be away from her girls, and it wasn't an act, but I think she also played it up a little, for what she probably thought was my sake. I couldn't blame her. It was a situation where you couldn't quite put a foot right. She wanted children and she had them. I wanted a child and I didn't. It might balance out at some point. Maybe David and I would, somehow, someday, have a child. There were still avenues, other than those we'd already been down, that David and I had discussed but those discussions were immersed in exhaustion and trepidation and, ultimately, postponement: *we could . . . at some point . . . maybe.* Perhaps the balancing would come when we were old, older, when Liz was out of the thick of it, when her children had left home. But where would any of us be by then?

They brought wine and beer and a berry pie or tart from a bakery I was supposed to have heard of. I directed them through the kitchen and out back to where David and Stella were. The introductions were warm and friendly but I caught Liz looking Stella up and down. It was a subtle assessment, but comprehensive. Liz had gotten what she needed, it seemed, and then—excitedly, without a moment to lose!—she asked for a tour of the house, while Felix expressed no such interest. And so it was the two of us in the kitchen, Liz opening a bottle of prosecco, pouring two glasses and handing one to me, and I sensed that Liz had a plan. She was, at the very least, onto

something, after something, and even though I was techni-
cally giving her the tour and she was following me, she was in
the lead.

Soon she was in our bedroom, just as Stella had been during
the storm and before my interview, except not just as Stella had
been. There was no mystery with Liz, there was no heightened
sensitivity, no subtle, ongoing negotiation. Liz had always had
a kind of innate authority, and therefore a certain presump-
tuousness that Stella didn't have. The way she occupied space
was different from Stella, who seemed to want to make a home
where she could. Stella wanted a nest while Liz simply wanted
a perch. Wanted to orient herself, her body, only temporarily.
The stakes were lower, it was easier, not as unnerving. It made
me happy to watch Liz move about these rooms, my room,
even to ham it up, draping her upper body like a jaguar along
the top of an upholstered wing chair, louche, champagne flute
in hand.

"So . . . Stella came with the place?" she asked.

I laughed, unsure what to say.

"I need someone like that," Liz said, casting Stella as a
live-in assistant, which threw me because Liz was usually correct in her assessments of the world. She wasn't always kind or
complimentary but she was generally right.

"It's not . . ." I said.

"At all like that movie?"

"What movie?"

She couldn't immediately come up with the name—
black and white, psychosexual, she said—and I understood

she meant *The Servant*, which we'd seen together in a college course on—what?—postwar decay of the British class system? London, early '60s. An aristocratic man hires a butler with murky motives, whose hold on him grows and deepens. Hierarchies get subverted, desire twisted, roles reversed. Order is not restored—something was rotten with that order to begin with. What stuck with me was the visual tone: insinuating, dark, all of it suffused with a kind of humid malignancy.

"She doesn't work for me," I said. Obvious, stupid. Not just because it was a fact, but because it was a simple answer to a simple question Liz didn't ask. The real question involved an interrogation into the very meaning of work—and control, power, deference, surrender. And I wanted to say there was none of that at play here. But there was. Of course there was. Stella choosing which clothes I should wear to my interview, performing a service, helping me, but at the same time determining what I would look like, how the world would see me. She was my Pygmalion. And I'd asked her to be. I'd placed myself in her skilled hands with their deep blue nails.

"Don't get defensive," said Liz. "I'm just curious. That's all."

"I think you're turning all of this into something more fevered than it is."

"I need someone to live vicariously through. It's true. I'm asleep by ten every night now. So, what I'm saying is do it for me."

"Do what?"

"I don't know. Use your imagination."

I'd been with her up to this point, enjoying it on some level, pleased at being the subject of some intrigue. But when she said this, it stirred distaste—for how she'd reduced Stella to an object for her own, for our own, amusement. How I'd reduced her, as well.

"Okay, Madame de Merteuil." I passed it off. We'd seen those movies too. The faithful eighteenth-century versions of *Les Liaisons Dangereuses* and the late-twentieth-century retelling with Upper East Side adolescents, now a period piece itself. I'd written part of my undergraduate thesis on the book, in French—Liz was there for it, though there's no way she'd remember the arguments I tried to advance about the letters of those manipulative libertines. I barely recall the terms I used, but I do remember I wanted to draw out connections between pedagogy and power, education and sex. And I knew that I was the Vicomte de Valmont in this scenario that Liz wanted to put us in: the seducer who gets seduced into caring. The one who drops his mask too soon.

"Where's David in all this?" she asked, and I wasn't sure I knew. Sometimes David and Stella were like those husbands in the Cassavetes movie. But I'd also been thinking of David and Stella—I realized as I told her—like people who meet and get to know each other in a support group they're attending because they've each got a loved one with the same problem. By that logic, the loved one was me. But what was my problem?

Her laugh was a kind of answer, I suppose. She'd changed

positions, now sitting in the wing chair, her legs pulled up, the arches of her feet on the piped edge of the seat cushion, toes pointed, her chin resting on her knees. Avid, assessing. Her glass on the floor, in need of refilling. I had only taken a few sips from mine.

"It's just . . ." she said. "I get it. You get to be someone new when you're seen by someone new. You know what I mean? Really seen. And I think that's what you miss and what you want at a certain age, when most of your firsts are behind you."

You want discovery, I thought, but I didn't say it out loud.

"Are you and Felix, like, not in a good place?" I asked.

She reached for her glass, frowned at its emptiness, then shrugged.

"Oh, we're fine. Really."

I didn't quite buy her breezy tone and my doubt must have registered on my face.

"We're good." She sighed. "But I can sort of feel a shift coming, in me."

For some reason I thought of elephants, sensing seismic waves through their feet. A distress call, an underground rumbling otherwise undetectable.

I once saw a piece that Liz had choreographed, in which a woman in a leotard and a wrap skirt performs a series of volatile movements not to music, exactly, but to a tape track of repeated, truncated yells. As if the full, original yell was lost or suppressed and all that remained was this found, spooky fragment. A dance critic included Liz's work in a round-up review, praising its evocation of "female rage" and speculating that its "somewhat obscure title"—*Dishes*—referred to "what is dished out" or perhaps to housework, or to "dishing" and the role of gossip in female subjectivity. I suppose it was all those things but I also knew where this dance came from, the source material it transformed. Liz and I had lived together in an apartment for a time after college and I came home to find her in the kitchen, in a fury, clacking together the porcelain plates that had been drying on the rack, almost throwing them on top of each other and then shoving the stack in the cupboard before slamming the door. Then she enacted similar violence on the cutlery drawer. She hadn't heard me come in or call her name.

When I asked what had set her off she had said it was "nothing." It was the "stupid fucking yapping dog downstairs" and the couple that played "loud as fuck" video games somewhere above us, a letter about her student loans, a passive-aggressive voice mail from her mother, a stubborn canker sore in her mouth. A whole litany of nothing that oppressed her only when it was compounded by something else, some lack of control she had over her life. But she wouldn't or couldn't tell me what that something else was. Instead, I suppose, she extracted it and made it into a dance. I never saw her seized like that again.

Before she could tell me more about this shift coming on, we were being called, from downstairs. David's voice. Liz didn't float down the staircase, that would have been too much, but she had a way of near-gliding, a lightness on her feet, a melody almost. She reached the bottom, not waiting for me, while I stopped on the landing, where the window looked out to the backyard. A rectangle of green, Stella in the far upper-right corner, Felix tossing something metal and weighted in her direction, David out of the frame. It took me a minute to interpret the image, to understand they were playing horseshoes. That's what the iron stake in the ground toward the trees was for. I'd passed it before and vaguely wondered, but never enough to investigate. The horseshoes came from where? Under the porch, the athletics shed, a corner of forgotten things in the lodge? Liz entered the picture with what I can only describe as efficiency, getting to the point, and the point was this: she took no interest in the horseshoes, she took little interest in Felix just then, her interest was in Stella, whom she didn't consider a rival, more like a gem whose facets had caught her eye, that she was selecting for closer inspection, for how it might look on her. She was establishing a line between herself and Stella that hadn't been there before but could now intersect or connect to all of the other lines that had been drawn.

And here's what I still didn't know about Stella—how aware was she of what Liz was doing? When Liz offered Stella her arm and Stella linked hers through, smiling modestly, and they exited the frame, while Felix remained, gathering the horseshoes in a tidy pile, was she oblivious or was she playing into the role Liz had given her? And then, if she was playing into it, how much was she subverting that role through her performance? And then I wondered, what was it like to have Liz for a mother?

David was at the foot of the stairs. Emily? he said. Snapping me back. Could I help him, he asked. Sorry, yeah, of course, sorry, I said. I followed him, taking his instruction—what we should bring out, what to serve at the start—because I still wasn't completely there.

But they'd made it look wonderful—David and Stella; Felix, too—inviting, easy. The wooden table, set with dishes and glassware, would fit us comfortably. We all assembled on the porch. The light at that time of day, in that spot, flattered everyone, and the mood was one of abundance—of good company and a good meal to come, of generosity, gratitude. We toasted to it and I was glowing, pleased and proud that David and I could offer this.

We ate, talked, drank. Like a camera lens refocusing, the specifics of the conversation blurred, but the sound of engaged voices, voices I loved, grew more defined, along with the breeze rustling the trees, the sound of the cutlery against the plates. Liz no longer seemed so full of orchestration or calculation. She seemed to be in the same flow of talk that David and Felix and Stella were in.

I readjusted. The topic of the conversation returned front and center—they were talking about music. The venue in the city where Stella had worked. Felix had gone there a lot, years ago, in his twenties. And I worried this would turn toward self-satisfied nostalgia—but when Felix recalled an "incredible" show he once saw there, there was nothing smug or patronizing about it. Only a remaining vitality strong enough that Stella went a little rapt, as if she could hear the sound, could feel it, reverberating in that space. Not like a child or a student being taught, but a fellow practitioner, nodding in understanding, identifying with. "They don't phone it in. My ears were ringing for days," he said. Stella smiled.

And I shouldn't have worried with Felix, who was genuine, though not unthinking, in his enthusiasms. He wore his intellect so lightly you could forget it was there, I felt, and I didn't mean it in an arch or bitchy way. I meant it less as a reflection on Felix than on people around him, who almost had to be told, brought up to speed, and only then would they acknowledge his intelligence, the kind of sly subtlety that doesn't announce itself, a depth of feeling that doesn't dramatize itself. I'm sure Felix had agonized over things in his life, but he never led with that agony, never wrapped himself up in it like a coat for the world to see. All of us at the table seemed to recognize this about Felix, and value it.

I knew that Liz, especially, recognized Felix for who and what he was without having to be told. She loved that such an intelligence was there in Felix and she loved that it wasn't the type to compete with hers. What was the shift she felt coming, the one she brought up earlier? Wouldn't Felix shift with her? Or accommodate her shift in some way? But I glimpsed it for a second—Felix, always gathering the horseshoes until one day he stops. He doesn't toss one at her back, nothing so violent. More than rage, there's resignation—he just leaves them there for Liz to pick up for once in her life and he walks away. And this, I suppose, was the problem. Liz wanted to rage at him so he would rage at her, but he simply didn't have that rage in him.

Still, I didn't really know what their life was like and I didn't want these thoughts. I wanted us to stay in the stream of good feeling. Of plenitude and ease in the last of the daylight. Where I could look at David and then meet his eyes and, in that moment, feel that nothing and no one was missing.

After second helpings we were full, but there was ice cream and sorbet for dessert and the pie-tart that Liz and Felix brought. I got up to serve it, feeling the wine in me, mixing with that glow from the start of the evening, dimmed a little bit now. I could have broken a dish, sent a few spoons clattering to the floor, dropped a carton of ice cream, and it wouldn't have mattered much. It would have merely become part of the flow of that night. But there was something about the pie-tart, I felt I had to take special care with it. That something vague but irretrievable would be lost if I messed it up. As ably as I could, I set it down whole in front of Liz and asked her to do the honors.

When she cut into it, the filling that squelched out was such a deep, dark red it had to symbolize something, but what? All the obvious analogies were boring so I said nothing, but I was delighted when she gave the first piece to me, as if it were my birthday.

So I brought it up, the cusp I was on. I mentioned the job interview, which Stella dressed me for (thank you, Stella, I nodded) and David had been supportive of (thank you, David). Felix and Liz said something along the lines of *oh, that's great!* And then I went into a little more detail, because at my age and with my experience a job interview shouldn't have been a big deal, but I wanted them to know it was not nothing to me. Not just the prospect of a job, of being employed, but the interview itself—having the chance (because it felt like chance) to successfully participate in a world I was beginning to think was no longer mine, would never be mine again. Maybe I went too far with this, conversationally. Felix still thought it was all great, but Liz shifted in her seat. She placed her elbow on the table, her chin jutting into her palm, her face arranged in a kind of pouting skepticism and concern.

"What is it?" I said to her.

"Oh, it's not . . . I don't know."

"What?"

"It sounds good, this opportunity. And I'm not saying you shouldn't get your hopes up. You should! And they'd be lucky to hire you. But I just think maybe you should apply to some temp agencies in the meantime. Or do some gig economy thing. Or try to reactivate your old contacts and freelance?"

I couldn't argue with the soundness of her suggestions, and I fully expected everyone to second, third, and fourth her, but her advice was loaded with a kind of judgment and superiority I wouldn't have expected from her. Or rather: I'd completely expect it from her, I just wouldn't have expected her to direct it toward *me*, to my face. The fact that I didn't anticipate anybody sensing how wounded it left me made my heart beat faster when Stella spoke, when she said to Liz:

"Why, though? Why should she?"

"Well, Stella," Liz said, elbow still on the table, chin still in hand, "money aside, it can't be good in terms of mental health for Emily to be wandering around here all day alone."

"But I'm not alone," I said.

Liz didn't reply, but I knew her well enough to see—she sat up straight, pulling back—that what I said had landed just as I'd wanted: she was baffled, jealous, a little put upon. And why not? Wouldn't she have liked to live in this idyll, to pass her days like this, in a haze of desire and memory, and a kind of physicality that drew on that haze, that energized it? When Stella and I swam, when we played tennis, rode our bikes, pumped our legs, swung our arms, our bodies knew everything, they could do everything. Everything I asked my body to do, it did. Liz, of all people, a dancer, would have understood this. Would have wanted it for herself. Her body may finally have belonged only to her again, after pregnancy and breast-feeding, but even so, most of the time she had was not her own. She taught a few university classes at different schools and she took care of her children. If she danced, I thought, more spitefully than sadly, it was a cramped, unsatisfying shadow version of both the freedom and control she had once possessed.

I looked from Liz to Stella, who showed no satisfaction at having challenged Liz, only concern. Whether it was concern for me or concern that she'd overstepped, I couldn't tell. But I wanted to let her know that she hadn't overstepped, or if she had, I didn't mind. I felt flush with shame at the way I'd let Liz talk about her earlier, the extent to which I'd gone along with it, and flush with gratitude—something more than gratitude—for Stella, for the way she cared.

Felix, who wasn't drinking much this evening, since he planned to drive home, attempted to come to Liz's rescue, to the whole table's rescue—to get us back to the convivial place we were before. He tried his best. He was unemployed for seven months once, he said, and loved it. He got my situation, he did. But then—I could see him actively reassessing his situation—this was before they had kids, he said. Before he was solidly with Liz, even. Before he cared about health insurance. And what he stopped himself from saying was that it was before he had to be responsible to anyone other than himself. The implication wasn't hard to decipher: I was selfish and irresponsible.

After a momentary but infinitely awkward silence, David spoke, as if from a dais, out to the waiting audience. "When we moved here, it was for a number of reasons, but part of what motivated us was a creative impulse. And maybe that sounds self-indulgent, or privileged or whatever, but if you give yourself that kind of license, it's hard to just shut it off. We'll probably have to make some decisions soon, and maybe sell this place. But right now, if you wanted to get a temp job"—he looked at me—"that's fine, but you don't need to, we don't need you to." His "we" was exclusionary, incorporating Stella but shutting out Liz and Felix, who apparently *did* need me to get a temp job in order to justify their own choices to themselves.

"Stop. This is making me sad." Liz lifted her gaze to mine. "You make us sound sad."

I got up and walked over behind her, a little swoony from

the wine. I poured what was left of the bottle into her glass, an offering, and standing by her chair, I kissed the crown of her head. "Don't be sad." She leaned back to meet my eyes, upside down, blinking, then smiling. A look I'd seen her give her children, a smile that spanned and compressed time, so that her own childhood wasn't behind her and her children's future ahead in a chronological, linear progression. It was all there at once, surging.

As I raised my head, I saw Stella pick up her glass and then put it down without drinking. She glanced at David, who was pouring water for Felix, she absently twisted the napkin in her lap, and then when she looked at me almost reluctantly, I thought just maybe I caught a flicker of jealousy.

The small white plates around the table, smeared with half-eaten pieces of pie, seemed to be keeping everyone there, in place, and if I removed them to the kitchen counter, I'd be removing a pin, releasing everyone, they'd go off in any direction they chose. Which didn't sound like a bad idea. We could make it a game, now that it was dark. Hide and seek. We could set as boundaries the edge of the playing field and the lodge, to the north and south, the tennis court and the rec hall to the east and west, and within them run off into the night.

Everyone, it turned out, was up for it. They'd hide, I would seek. We set rules: twenty minutes and then you returned here if you hadn't been found. Phones for flashlights.

I closed my eyes, counted out time, and then I was off. Not quite stumbling but not sure-footed either. That forward, loping motion of almost letting yourself fall before you put your foot down, over and over. It was a clear night, the warmth of the day just beginning to surrender to a chill in the air. I didn't have a plan but I thought it would be so sweet to find David, as if there were an invisible cord between us and he could reel me toward him. And David was close by, I imagined, in a clever spot that didn't require too much effort for him to get to. An elegant solution, as usual. Liz would go far and not stop until she was out of breath. Felix, I didn't know about but I suspected him to be somewhere in the middle of our circumscribed area. And Stella? It was Stella I found.

A working security flood lamp on the side of the infirmary cast a cone of light into the darkness, bright enough to see a few fluttering moths, wide enough so that I could see Stella at the edge of its circumference, on the wooden steps of the building. Sitting with her elbows resting on her knees, her hands supporting her chin—a bored pose, but not necessarily a dissatisfied one. A minor rustling from somewhere underneath the bunk-like structure and the crack of a branch in the nearby pines seemed to cause her little concern.

"I tried to go in but it's locked," she said, as I approached and stood facing her. "You got me."

"You know, for someone who lived here undetected for weeks, you're surprisingly bad at hiding."

"I made it easy for you." She blinked but kept looking right at me. And then she shrugged and smiled. I still didn't know how to take her tone. The way she seemed to have of making statements that were, on one level, completely literal and straightforward, but which also suggested another level. A beguiling one. I kept standing there because I wasn't exactly sure what we were supposed to do now—should I walk her back to headquarters like a prize horse?

What I did was thank her, for defending me at the dinner table.

"Is that what I was doing?"

"It's always been so easy with them, Liz and Felix. I thought it would be tonight. I'm sorry."

Stella didn't say anything but I could hear her, or else it was my own inner voice: *You thought it would be easy?*

"I don't know," I said, answering myself, out loud.

"Don't know what?" Stella asked.

"Why I do some of the things I do."

She looked at me like a skeptical child. Or a tired psychotherapist.

"Thanks for inviting me to the . . ."—she searched for the word—"party."

"Of course."

And I realized only just then that I had orchestrated this whole evening not at all *for* Stella but *around* her. I wanted her to meet Liz and Felix not because I thought they'd all get along so well, but because I wanted to show Stella off and then see what that would do to Liz. Not the same, not at all the same as Liz presenting her children, her life, to me. But I'm not sure the motivation was entirely different. And I also hadn't known that I'd wanted to see what Liz's presence would do to Stella.

I sat down beside her on the steps as if I needed some stability to comprehend this more fully but I didn't dwell on the thought. Instead, I thought back to my friend Berrie, when we were counselors here and would sit out on bunk steps just like this in our sweatshirts, talking in low voices because our campers were supposed to be sleeping. In my memory, Berrie had always been frank and free and unembarrassed. But now I remembered it differently, how when she would tell me about times with John the kitchen guy, going off into the woods with him, she was completely open with me, but she would also drop her already quiet tone to a theatrical whisper whenever she said things like "blow job" or "dick" or "finger." The vocal equivalent of blushing.

I started talking, as if Stella had read my thoughts, as if no connective words were needed. "I have this sense," I said, "that younger people, and it makes me feel so old to even say that, but that as a generation now, they have no hang-ups about sex. They're just fine with everything, I mean as long as it's consensual. Which is great, you know? But how is it even really possible? Like, I have hang-ups—hesitation, self-consciousness, shame—about interactions I have with people in *grocery stores*. Did that 'excuse me' come out right? Was I too chatty or not chatty enough with the cashier? It's not crippling or anything, I go buy food when I need to, but it's there, even in a situation that's so low-stakes. God, how do you not have that with people you're having *sex* with? How are you all so comfortable in your skin?"

"You're making a sweeping generalization." Some

amusement in her voice. But also some uncertainty. She looked down at her knees.

"You're not answering my question."

I looked down at her knees. They were just knees. A safe focal point.

"What younger people are you talking about? I mean, aside from me, what younger people do you know?" She lifted her gaze, shifted slightly closer to me.

"I don't know. People I see online or whatever."

"Well. I don't know what to say. You feel bad about having hang-ups?"

"I think I just wish I were more fearless about things." I was talking, at this point, to fill up space, to postpone what felt like an inevitability.

"It's not like it's all one thing or all one way. If I'm going to represent young people everywhere, online and off, I'd have to say, yeah, there are people who are comfortable in their own skin, fine with everything. But those people aren't the ones telling you how comfortable in their own skin they are. The people who do that, who make an effort to show you how fine they are with everything, are usually the most *uncomfortable*, with the most to prove. And it's not so much about age. Or so it seems to me."

"You're very smart," I said, slurring the "very" a little but tightening up the "smart." A drunk exaggeration of being drunk. And she accepted the compliment, though I didn't know whether she took it seriously.

But now the outside of her right knee was touching the outside of my left, and then my face found hers, or hers found mine. *I made it easy for you.* We kissed, we were kissing. Later, when I was sober, I would wonder why, why any of it, but the moment was all sensation. Pressure and release, some stain of sweetness still on her lips from the tart Liz brought. My head had no room for thought, only a kind of movement that seemed involuntary. All of it was present-tense and not-in-time, or it was *all* time—Liz's face when she'd looked up at me earlier at dinner, me sitting on steps like this with Berrie—until a very delicate balance shifted and structured the moment into a narrative: beginning, middle, end.

Stella pulled back, moved to her feet. She had her hand to her lips. She wouldn't look at me.

"Stella—"

"I'm sorry," she said. Meeting my eyes for the briefest moment, pushing her hands into her pockets.

I could feel myself becoming that person who wanted to acknowledge and analyze everything. A kind of defense mechanism, even in my intoxication—to intellectualize what was happening, as if that would make what was happening any better or easier. The person who, if this were a play, if it were performance art, would force us to confront ourselves right now, force an exegesis. The type of play where we'd even talk about why we were talking about it. Self-awareness as a hall of mirrors to run down or to smash. Either way, though, you were ultimately left in that hall, and I didn't want to be in that hall. I wanted to be on those steps, I wanted her to return with me to that fluidity—the wine, the kiss, our bodies, time itself. I wanted impossible things.

My phone lit up with a message. From Liz. They'd all returned to the porch, they were wondering if we were okay.

"Shit," I said.

"I think I'm going to head home, to the bunk. It feels late and I work early tomorrow. Will you just tell them all good night for me?"

"Sure, but—" But what? I couldn't complete the thought. I only nodded, though she'd already turned away, disappearing into the dark, until all I could see was the white light from her phone and then not even that.

I replied monosyllabically to Liz—"Be there soon." This, too, had become a scene with a beginning, middle, and end.

We didn't play another round. We went inside, to golden lamp-light in the living room, where Liz and Felix started talking about their kids. Their default, what they usually talked about in the company of other adults they knew, aside from us, and they let down whatever guard had been up in Stella's presence. They sat in chairs, on either side of the fireplace, that faced each other, while David and I were together on the couch, listening, but it was like listening to exit music. We were all on our way out.

Up in our room, David told me my lips were stained, as if I'd been drinking red wine. But I'd only had white that evening.

It was that dessert, I said. Whatever was in it. Red as blood. Revivifying. No wonder that bakery had long lines.

We kissed, a shallow, routine, good night kiss in bed, but I held on to him, kissed him deeply now, continuously, and it was a continuation of that depth when he was inside me.

PROBABILITIES

I woke the next day, mid-morning, uncharacteristically full of determination and pluck. It was the weekend—I wasn't going to hear anything more about the job with Samira today, so I could stay suspended in a state of hopefulness. Optimistic enough, even, to think that if it didn't work out, there would be other options to come. I would make other options appear. I'd root around my bag of tricks and pull out a plan. What adults do.

"You don't sound exactly like an adult," said David. "You sound like a magician or a character in a musical who's going to burst into song about rejoining the workforce."

"Just you wait!"

"But I did mean what I said last night."

"I know. But I feel like I need to start pulling my weight."

"Why start now?"

His perfect timing. His straight face undone first by his eyes, which triggered the rest of his features to subtly give way. If this kind of conversation, this tone, was a dodge, a means of not taking things seriously, it was also the opposite of a dodge—it pinned us down, held us there, contained us. It allowed for the unspoken expression of something that couldn't be more serious. Something you didn't see—the deep-dug foundation—without which you couldn't build upper levels that were open and light. Irony in its most generous, most capacious, most necessary form. What I didn't say, but what coalesced in this conversation—what I realized for the first time—was that I had been out these past months on a sort of delayed nonmaternity leave. In a way, I *had* been pulling my weight, and his, if you thought of the weight as grief. David would never have pushed me to go back, but I could feel this time beginning to come to an end. Or transform, at least. That is, I could conceive of it as a time, finite.

Liz hadn't been wrong about me the night before, with her stated concern for my mental health, but she had been coming from the wrong place.

Was it strange that I didn't feel guilt or remorse or even much responsibility for kissing Stella? That I wasn't sitting at the table, staring into my coffee cup, on edge? That instead I was enjoying my coffee, that this cup of coffee couldn't have been better, as I sat there with David. The events of the evening before were still hanging around, albeit in a modified form, like water that had evaporated and condensed into a harmless cloud that was already moving along, off into the distance. Or so it seemed.

The only impending source of tension that Sunday morning was a deadline David had, a time-sensitive project that would require him to work that day, from home. And I understood how hard it was to work with someone else in the house, the silent riot your mind takes up against that person, a kind of chant: *When are you going to leave? Why haven't you left? Fucking go!* He didn't have to ask—I would head out, go down to the lake. I'd bring a book for the beach, pack a lunch, swim out to the floating dock, write cover letters in my head. I didn't have to think about running into Stella and what I might do or say; she had told me that her shift started early today. She didn't lie, she wasn't a liar. Or else she was the best liar in the world.

Trees lined the wide, worn path down to the water, creating a high canopy of shade. A breeze cut through the day's early humidity. Everything was old but everything was also renewed. I remembered the dream I had—the lake extending out into another lake. Good fortune.

As an adult, I never swam all that much or regularly before we came to Alder, but I had since become strong and smooth in the water. I could go and go and not tire. I swam out to a deep, cool spot and floated on my back so all I saw was blue sky and the green pines. Shouts from the other side, land dotted by houses, reached me every now and then. I knew the few families that lived across the lake by sight, to say hello to in town, but no more than that. To my knowledge, there wasn't any enforced rule preventing them from swimming or boating close to camp, but none of them ever did. The middle of the lake, though, felt like international waters. As a young camper, I had been afraid of this depth, where the water was so dark it was almost black. I worried about snapping turtles and carnivorous fish that would bite off my foot. Those creatures didn't live here, I was told, but it didn't matter. How did anyone know for sure?

There are surprises and upsets and things you never saw coming. But what about the thing you did see coming, the highly unlikely thing that you weren't supposed to spend time worrying about? Had I been attacked by a snapping turtle in this lake it would have been an extraordinary event but I couldn't have said I didn't expect it. Stella. What was Stella? What were the odds of me finding her here at Alder? Her presence, that day I first saw her in the bunk, hadn't shocked me. I hadn't seen her coming, but I had seen her absence, felt it so keenly that I wondered if I hadn't imagined her into being what I needed.

Which was what? Newness, maybe. It wasn't fair or correct to say there was nothing new between David and me, simply because we'd known each other a long time. It was always familiar, but not always comfortable. Because we'd known each other for a long time, we knew, somatically, when something was up. Our changing moods, our thoughts, our concerns—it all registered and came through in our bodies. With Stella, I could only guess. And with Stella, it was the newness that got me. I wanted her newness, but I also wanted my own newness back. We had lost potential—I had lost potential, lost some sense of possibility that I had taken for granted, some underlying, grounding idea of who I was and who I would be—and I didn't know how to come to terms with that. How to gracefully accommodate that. I didn't want to think of our existence, mine and David's, as a long process of diminishment, but what else was it, really? And then Stella had appeared.

It embarrassed me, thinking of what I'd said to her on the steps the night before about sex and hang-ups. I wasn't even sure what I'd meant, other than the fact that she made me feel uneasy in a way I'd stopped being conscious of. If I had ever been uneasy with David, in that charged, almost repressed way, time had taken care of it long ago. We got up off that bench at Brighton Beach. We got to know each other.

Something passed beneath me that I couldn't see, rippling by my toes, sending a shudder through me, but I kept floating, in the sun and the dark water. Uncle Joe had wondered what the fuck was wrong with people who didn't like a lake, and he would sit on the beach in a folding chair of woven plastic strips, appreciating the view, occasionally wading in. But it was Aunt Esther who couldn't live without the water. As a ritual, she would go for a swim at dawn, before the camp was awake, often turning up at breakfast with her hair, grown long in the '70s and kept long for years, in a wet braid. I remember her swimming out once, so far, beyond and behind the island. The lake empty except for the two of us. But when would this have happened? Just the two of us there? What I remember is this: me, on the dock, in a green bathing suit I can date to age

eleven, reading-but-not-reading a book, the backs of my legs
pressing, ever more anxiously, into the corrugated metal, when
I could no longer see her, the pressure letting up only when
she came back into view. I had always thought, whenever I'd
landed on this memory, that I was worried for her, but she was
a good swimmer. I was worried for myself. Being left there
alone. She climbed the ladder on the dock, revitalized, while I
quietly ran my hands up and down the marks on my legs. She
drew her towel about herself and then came over and wrapped
her arms around me from behind, her wet cheek on mine,
drops of water on the pages of my book.

I don't know, thinking back, if there was anything conscious or intentional on Aunt Esther's part in leaving me there
alone. I never told her I was afraid, she never said she knew.
But I wondered now, as I swam in and pulled myself up the
ladder onto the dock, if she was testing my mettle. On the
other hand, maybe she wasn't thinking about me or my mettle
at all as she went for her swim. Either way, it struck me as a
kind of lesson.

I ate my lunch on a blanket, read part of one book and
then part of another, and by the time I returned to the house,
it was late afternoon. I didn't have work I had to go back to the
next day, but I still had that end-of-Sunday feeling that's been
with me since elementary school. A feeling not unlike the one
I had as a child on the dock. A letting-go and a tightening grip,
a gearing-up. A lonely feeling.

"Back here," said David when I called to him. He was at
the kitchen table, on his computer, papers spread out. And I

noticed, too, a plastic, logoed cup of iced coffee, almost gone, from the place where Stella worked. David's name along the side of it, in writing that looked a lot like that girlish, tall, looping hand of Stella's.

"I needed a change of scene," he said, answering a question I didn't ask.

"Yeah, totally." Making an effort to be nonchalant. Exactly the kind of effort, the slight betrayal of tone, that David would recognize. But he didn't push me on it. And I wasn't immediately sure what I was trying to be nonchalant about.

So he went to the coffee shop to work and saw Stella there. The two of them without me. So what? My head didn't start spinning but I felt the immediate urge to shut myself up alone in a room upstairs so that it could do just that.

"Well, I'll let you keep working," I said, and before I knew it, I was in the glossy green-tiled bathroom upstairs, sitting on the edge of the white tub, my chin digging into my palms, elbows into knees.

Did Stella tell him about our kiss? A kiss, nothing to lose your head over. But still. Is this what I deserved for thinking I could get away with it, with kissing her and suffering no consequences? Or did she not even have to tell David because he already knew? Like the two of them were in on this? But in on what? Was something happening between the two of them? Something I had missed, mistook for good-natured fellow-feeling? In *Husbands* the wives are nothing, that is, they have almost no screen time, other than a few images, by a pool, with children, one sequence of domestic violence. When

I thought of David and Stella that way, with a shared, deep but platonic understanding, why did I assume that left any room for me? But . . . but what if I was wrong about that, too, and Stella was working both of us? But why, what for? I couldn't ascribe a motivation to her, though the suspicion was suddenly there. As was a vulnerability—I'd left myself open to being taken advantage of, and I'd pulled David into it, and what had I done?

I wasn't sure that I became any wiser as I got older. Increasingly, there was that creeping sense of not catching on. Of being aware there was something to catch on to and missing it. Or thinking something was a parody, that it must be, only to eventually realize it was not. That there was no longer any face value at which to take things.

"Em?" David was in the upstairs hallway. I stopped the spiraling, pulled myself together.

"Yeah?"

"You okay?"

"I'm fine, yeah. I'll be right out."

We stood in the narrow, dusky hall and I put my hands on his shoulders and looked in his eyes—because we knew each other's body. It was a coffee cup with his name on it in her handwriting. It was a drunk kiss on the infirmary steps. That's it. That's all.

He reminded me how bright and shiny I had been that morning, and I told him how long ago that seemed.

"How's your work?"

"Good. I'm in good shape. It was good to have the day."

Good, good, good.

"Did you see Stella at the coffee place?"

"Yeah, she says hi. She thanked me, us, for dinner."

"Really? I was worried dinner was too much, with Liz and everything."

"Yeah. You know, one of the things I love about Liz is that it always seems like she's got some kind of agenda. And it's great if you're into her agenda, it gives things purpose, something to be engaged in and working toward. She kind of demands that you be into it, though. And you and I always go along. But I think Stella's attitude was more along the lines of *fuck no.*"

He said *fuck no* and it punctured all pretense, anything too mannered (Liz) or melodramatic (my overwrought bathroom thought-spasm). It opened a window in that hothouse and, for a moment, fresh air rushed in and I experienced that rush as an actual physical sensation. A lighter heart, lungs filled with oxygen.

THREE WOMEN

Monday arrived and with it the expectancy that I might hear something about the job, a message from Samira or Jenna confirming a follow-up meeting. *More soon.* I had put all my eggs into this basket—the only basket I had. But nothing was coming through and I couldn't sit there all day hitting refresh. I had no distractions preventing me from seeing Stella and accounting for my actions on Saturday night. Was I supposed to apologize? I thought I was supposed to, but that was before David's name in her handwriting on a coffee cup kicked up my swirling suspicions and doubts. But I wondered if those suspicions and doubts were merely an excuse, a way for me to mitigate whatever I'd done, with her, to her, to David, to all of us. It was all a jumble now but I was certain that when I saw her, things would be reordered, clarified somehow.

I didn't exactly know her schedule, but Monday mornings she was often around. I would go to her bunk and not over-think it. No rehearsing. No looking in the mirror before I left the house.

I focused on the line of the dark green treetops, where they met the sky, which was so blue and cloudless. Some small part of me wanted to be shot off into it and not come back. To disappear into that endless blue curtain. It was dizzying, so I looked ahead, toward the bunk. But before I reached it, before anyone had seen me approaching, the cabin door opened and out walked a woman, shaking out her long, curly hair, and then turning, stretching her body to the sun. She was naked. Her hair fell down her back. She had large but high breasts, ample hips, fleshy yet firm thighs, like a Renaissance painting of a classical goddess. It was Alice. I recognized her from the pictures on Stella's phone. She looked like she owned the place. And for a moment, she did.

Stella appeared then, behind her, on the front steps, in a T-shirt and Aunt Esther's silk robe, hanging open, over it. Alice pulled on the hem of the T-shirt, like *why do you have this thing on?* I couldn't make out what they were saying but there was laughter before Stella went back inside.

I realized I'd witnessed this while ducking into shrubbery. This felt emblematic of a larger issue, representative of my character. It was pure slapstick. I couldn't take myself seri-ously enough. How could you take yourself seriously enough when you were hiding behind a bush? It reminded me of the conversation I'd had with Stella about how Alice didn't give a fuck. You have to take yourself seriously, on a certain level, in order to not give a fuck. To not give a fuck about being "nice," wanting to be liked. But "liked" was a complicated concept, especially for women. There were women who didn't give a fuck about being "nice," but they certainly cared about being esteemed and envied. They cared about their status, in the way a celebrity must, and so, as celebrities did, they created a persona. What they didn't give a fuck about was how canny and calculating anyone might think they were in their desire for admiration, in creating roles for themselves to fill, images to represent those roles. It was not so far removed, I thought, while crouched behind this huckleberry bush, from the way Lucille LeSueur became Joan Crawford or Norma Jeane Mortenson became Marilyn Monroe, except they weren't products of the sexist Hollywood studio system. It was more subtle, much lower-key, more self-determining, potentially more subversive, but the difference was in degree, not in kind. Being a woman, in public, in the world, is a kind of Warholian project. The no-fucks women make it look easy, but it's one of the hardest things—to create a persona and then to live in it. How much of a fuck you actually have to give in order to not give a fuck! It's the trickiest game, and instead of trying and losing, I had never really played, I had never taken myself seriously enough to play. I heard "yeah, get in line, join the club" and I got in line. And when I got out of line, it was to come here, to a kind of seclusion, where I didn't have to be a woman in the world. But being here was ultimately only a kind of hiding.

It was enough. I was tired of it. I emerged from the hedge and stood there in the open field. If they saw me, they saw me. If they were too busy with each other, with their beautiful bodies, that would be fine, too. Alice didn't own this place; I did. And just then I didn't give a fuck.

Well, I gave enough of a fuck to have brushed the leaves off myself and maneuvered around the hedge so it wasn't obvious I'd been crouched within it. As if I'd come from another direction. But then I stood there in the open field and Alice spotted me. She held one hand to her eyes like a visor and raised the other in a kind of motionless wave before she let it fall into her messy hair. I didn't wave back, I slowly walked toward her, and she, barefoot, stepped down a little more eagerly onto the area of dirt and stones and patchy grass just below the cabin stairs, to meet me. Her blond-brown hair was long enough and thick enough to cover and reveal her breasts as she moved.

"Emily, right?" Her voice a little scratchy but mostly sonorous, mostly lovely.

I nodded.

"Alice?" I wasn't going to pretend I didn't know who she was.

We didn't shake hands and I think the reason was that she was naked. And though I was the one fully dressed and she had no clothes on, her nakedness humiliated me. It was meant to, at any rate. I'm pretty sure that's what she intended it to do—but of course she would never have admitted to that. What she would've said is that she was just naked, natural beneath the sun on a luminous day, and whatever shame or curiosity or envy that stirred in me was only a symptom of my repression. If I gave a fuck, I would've been humiliated.

"Stella told you about me, I guess," she said.

I could hear the shower running inside the bunk and I assumed Stella was in it.

"A little, yeah."

We were the same height. Alice fixed me with her gray-green eyes, almond-shaped and upturned. Her long face gave her a regal air but her blunt nose counteracted it, as did her manner. Casual, disheveled.

"She told me a little about you, too," Alice said.

There wasn't anything insinuating in her tone, I was surprised to find. She didn't seem to be hinting at anything. But whatever I'd heard from Stella led me to believe Alice had a ravenous, greedy mind. Or at least one that was always on, always running.

"I think it's really cool that you let her stay here," she added.

"Well, we've got a lot of space."

"I know," she said. "It's amazing. I just want to make, like, dandelion crowns and commune with the grass. Just roll all around in it. Or whatever."

"Yeah."

"So, were you coming to see Stella?"

"I was out walking, but yes, I thought I'd see if she was around."

She motioned for the two of us to head inside the bunk

and wait there for Stella to finish her shower. I'm not sure whether she simply didn't see this as intrusive or if she knew exactly how intrusive it was.

"Stella! Stella! Stella!" she bellowed, opening the cabin door. "We have company." The bathroom, with its peeling linoleum floor, was a straight shot down the center of the cabin from the front entrance. It was built with two working shower stalls and two toilets. I could see Stella's arm reaching to pull a towel off a hook and then she stepped out, all wrapped up, tucked in, clean and snug.

"Hi, Emily," she said, walking toward us. She didn't quite have the look of a child getting caught out by a parent but there was a trace of wrongdoing in her expression. *I'm not your mother*, I wanted to say. *Despite how old and uptight and parental Alice wants me to feel.*

Stella understood me somehow. *No, you're not my mother,* she communicated back. *More like a witness to my conscience.* And she tossed Alice a T-shirt, while she put Aunt Esther's robe over her towel, and then, once covered, pulled the towel out from beneath her and hung it on a nail.

Alice took the T-shirt Stella gave her and showily pulled it overhead. She gathered up the bottom hem around her lower ribs, then looped that gathered fabric through the neck line and tugged it down to make a kind of cropped bra top. Eventually, she found a pair of underwear. I remembered walking home from school, down a leafy suburban street on a hot day, just before the end of eighth grade with my friend Nina. We'd done the same thing with our shirts, and a neighbor lady, a homemaker, not like our mothers, drove by and looked askance at us. "Puritan bitch!" Nina called out after her car. It seemed to me, at the time, like the most Massachusetts of insults.

There were old striped mattresses on two of the twin iron-framed beds in this bunk. Stella's bed had sheets and the other now had a red sleeping bag unrolled on it. Alice lay back on it, staring up at the rafters, her arms folded behind her head, while I sat near Stella on her made-up bed and we both seemed to be trying not to look at Alice's breasts, lolling in their make-shift bra.

It was a while before anyone said anything, but then Stella asked after David, how his work was going, that she'd seen him and they'd talked a little the day before when he came in to get coffee.

"Good," I said. "His work is good. I think he's got it under control now."

"That's good."

Good, good, good.

"And have you heard anything about your interview?"

"No. Not yet."

At this, Alice sat up, perked up, and asked me the name of the company, so I told her and right away she grabbed her phone and found its site. Scrolling, nodding at the clothes.

"Nice," she said. "My mom would love this stuff. I'll have to tell her about it."

I tried to keep my expression neutral.

"But you want to work for them?" She sounded skeptical.

"I think I'd like to, yeah."

Her mouth scrunched up with more skepticism along with a little condescension, maybe even pity, for my small, insular, and unimaginative life. She didn't confine any of this to her mouth for long.

"There's just so much wrong right now, in our country, in the world, and there's so much to do, and it kind of breaks my heart that you"—pointing to Stella with her left hand—"spend your days making specialty coffee drinks for people and you"—pointing to me, right hand—"want to, what, sell clothes to people who like specialty coffees?"

Alice, do you not like clothes and specialty coffees? Do you not know what depression is? Has your body never failed you? Have you ever wanted something so much, and gotten so close you thought maybe it was really yours, and then it wasn't? It wasn't yours, it wasn't anyone's. It was gone.

"We were going to host refugees here," I said. Almost like a machine, like an old black computer screen filling with green lines of commands and code, and this line was the last and for some reason it was audible.

"Like give them a temporary home?"

"That was the idea. An idea. But we haven't been able to make it work. We can't fix this place up in the way we were hoping. We ran out of resources. So here we are. And I'm crossing my fingers I have the opportunity to sell clothes to your mom."

Stella laughed, Alice pouted.

"You'll be in your last year at college, right?" I asked her. I didn't give a fuck, so I could soften.

"That's right."

"And you're studying comparative literature?"

"Stella fully briefed you. Yeah."

"That was my major. That and film."

"Oh, yeah?" She readjusted her breasts. "What did you focus on?"

"I studied French as my other language. And then I wrote a thesis on female education. Education as seduction. Seduction as education. Pedagogy and power. In *Les Liaisons Dangereuses*, *Henry V*, and Hal Hartley's movie *Trust*."

"Hal Hartley is a man, I'm assuming?"

"Yes."

"Those are all by men."

"I think that was part of my point. Then I wrote a whole section on Hélène Cixous and *The Laugh of the Medusa*."

"Huh. Sounds very '90s."

"I suppose it was."

"Well, I haven't narrowed it down too much but right now I'm really interested in the intersection of labor, leisure, and love. Female labor, leisure, and love. In literature."

"That's a big intersection."

"Yes, lots of directions to go in. But I'm already getting tired of how theoretical it all gets, the circularity of it—I mean the circularity of writing theoretically, analytically. All these essays. You think you get to some breakthrough, but nothing really breaks. It's all in your head. Sometimes I just want to smash things."

"You could go into demolition," said Stella, just loud enough.

"Don't start," said Alice.

"What," I interjected. I wanted Stella to start in on Alice. And she did. Changing her position next to me on the bed, tucking her legs under her and leaning forward toward Alice. Not aware that her robe opened a little as she moved.

"It's just, Alice, you're really interested in labor as a concept or a conceptual framework, but you've never had an actual job."

Alice stayed where she was, gazing up at the rafters again.

"Stella, I'm sorry but your understanding of labor is so narrow."

"And my understanding of love?"

"I don't know. The way you think of love, it strikes me as sort of naive." Alice finally looked directly at Stella. "Like you see it as removed from any larger political or social context or structures and you always want to reduce it to its most personal level."

"Oh my god, Alice!" Stella laughed, so incredulous she was almost amused. "How can it not be personal?"

For a moment, I was no longer there. It was like watching a movie. One of the French films I'd been revisiting, where the characters go on vacation and have serious, somewhat philosophical conversations about love and desire. The light touch of the direction brings out the comedy of it all—but only for the viewer.

I was certain, just then, that Stella hadn't mentioned our kiss to Alice. If she had, Alice would likely have thrown it back at her in that moment. Not to accuse her of any kind of betrayal but rather to call her out on how predictable, how pedestrian it was. How in keeping it was with her naively personal, bourgeois notions of love.

Alice rifled through a backpack, found a pair of blue denim cutoffs, and pulled them on. High-waisted, fraying around her upper thighs.

There must have been so many moments like this when I went to camp here. Half-dressed girls, young women, lazing around the bunk. The kind of images you'd see in a film likely directed by a man, the camera lingering on their bodies, and proceed with your critique of the objectifying male gaze. When I was living inside those scenes, a half-dressed girl at camp, I never much looked at the other girls, at Berrie, for example, with what I understood at that time to be desire. If I lingered on their bodies it was mostly out of curiosity, comparing my own form to theirs. If it ever was desire, it was never enough to act on much beyond some kissing and clumsy groping in college. But the way I found myself looking at Alice and Stella did have to do with desire. And I looked at them with an objectifying gaze. Only it wasn't male. It wasn't even female. It had more to do with age objectifying youth.

"Fine," said Alice. "It's personal. If it wasn't personal, I wouldn't be here."

"Thanks for honoring me with your presence," said Stella.

"Come on. This is getting tedious. Can we go out somewhere? You'll get dressed and we'll get lunch? My treat, obviously, because I'm so fucking rich I've never had to have an actual job." I remembered Stella and David talking about their exes, how cheap they were, how Alice rarely paid for much of anything, always wanted free drinks. Alice stood by Stella's dresser now, picking up objects—the bottles of nail polish—and placing them back down. Stella rose, steered her away, and it was as though they only just then remembered I was still there. Without a word, Stella took her clothes and headed back to the bathroom, not wanting to dress in front of Alice now, or in front of me. "I'll pay for you, too, Emily," Alice said, and I imagined it was hardly the first time she relied on her money this way, as if it could smooth over an awkward situation and make her untouchable, unfazed. "Maybe you could drive us someplace?"

Alice had arrived here by commuter rail and a ride-share app. Stella only had her bike. David had taken our Honda to work that morning but we also had a camp vehicle, an old, manual transmission pickup truck here in the garage when we'd arrived and which we'd never driven off the property. "But why not?" I said. "I wouldn't trust it to make it to Boston, but it should be fine if we don't go too far."

In the boxy vehicle, Alice sat beside me, and Stella next to her. The three of us in a row behind the windshield. I had to keep reaching between Alice's knees for the gear shift. There was no air-conditioning, and if our skin touched, it stuck a little. Her legs were fixed in place, adhering to the tan vinyl interior. At first, we were silent. Then Alice started to make exaggerated sex noises every time my hand went for the mechanism. It was slapstick again—any eroticism was left back in the bunk—but this time, I wasn't the hapless one. I'd pulled them into it. Silence, moan, silence, rattled breath, silence, high-pitched cry. It went on like this until Alice had had enough and turned on the radio, which still worked along a dial. She tuned it to a soul song from the '70s, and danced in her seat. To the extent that I could see without taking my eyes off the road, Stella was nodding her head, staring out the passenger side window.

When we entered the Thai restaurant, an older couple was coming out, and they didn't hold the plate glass door for us. The man, wearing camo-patterned plastic shoes and belted khaki shorts, already had his aerodynamic sunglasses on, the lenses so dark I couldn't tell where he was looking. But the woman, blond in a fitted coral button-down, more than glanced at Alice—who still had her top revealingly twisted up—with contempt. I could see a little fear, too, in her eyes, but mostly contempt, and I wasn't sure the contempt was entirely for Alice. It was directed at me, as well. The kind of look that Liz had told me about, the judgmental parent at the playground.

"Puritan bitch," I said, under my breath. The woman didn't hear me but Alice and Stella did and I'm sure their cackles reached her before the door completely closed. I had read this man and woman as an older couple but we could very well have been around the same age. I wondered why they made themselves look the way they did, but I assume they wondered the same about me.

Alice and Stella faced me across a four-top. I couldn't tell whether I was their tribunal or they were mine. But neither

turned out to be the case. The dish of noodles that Alice ordered resembled her: overflowing, profuse. A soft heap that
could bury you. Dominant Alice who couldn't quite be contained by clothing. Gorgeous, slovenly Alice, slurping up
strands through her glistening lips. Stella and I ate our curries
but we also watched each other watching Alice and so there
were two currents coursing: one between Alice and her noodles and one between Stella and me. Despite the fact that Alice had presumably come for Stella, that they were still lovers,
nothing powerful seemed to be surging from one to the other.
The stronger current, the more significant one, was mine and
Stella's.

The last time I was here in this restaurant, with David,
was the evening of the day I took out Stella's splinter before
she biked away. When I couldn't bring myself to tell him about
her because she was so new and unexpected but not entirely
so that I hadn't even known what to say. All I could do was
excitedly order the kind of iced coffee I thought I no longer
had a taste for.

When Alice excused herself and headed to the restroom, it
was the first moment I'd had alone with Stella that day.

"Alice seems nice." I channeled David's deadpan.

Stella put her head in her hands and shook it right and left.

"She just showed up yesterday, with her sleeping bag."

"Out of the blue? You weren't in touch at all?"

"I don't know. No. We've been texting."

I think she expected me to scold her, for backsliding with
her ex, possibly. But that wasn't my inclination. Alice's presence

uncomplicated the situation—my situation—to an extent. Or complicated it in a way that relieved me of something—the weight of responsibility, maybe.

"Do you mind if she stays?" Stella asked. I hadn't even thought to exercise that say-so, that it was up to me, as an authority figure or a sort of landlord.

"How long do you think she'll be here for?"

"She wanted to get away for a few days before classes start up again."

That's what it was: Alice had resituated us in forward-moving time. She would go back to school. The summer would end. I would have watched all the movies I could. I would get a job. We would leave this place. David and I would move to Boston. And Stella . . . where would Stella go?

"That sounds fine," I said, just as Alice came back.

"Do you ever get stuck on the toilet?" Alice asked. "I mean, not literally, but like you're sitting there and you lose track? There's a painted-over graffito in there I was trying to make out. It looked like it said 'LIK ME.' Lick me? Like me?"

I laughed, and I liked Alice's use of the singular graffito.

"One of life's great mysteries," Stella said.

"You know it," said Alice.

When our bill came, Alice made no move to pick it up. Even when Stella offered me cash that I waved away as I placed my credit card in the check holder.

You see? Stella asked me silently.

I see. Alice, who had been to Bangkok and Phuket, was chatting with the co-owner, Mae, about a certain chili used in Thai cuisine, and their talk animated them both—elastic faces, involved hands—so that it was hard to interrupt them and also hard to fault Alice. There was something undeniable, unstanchable about her.

In the truck once again, our configuration repeated itself: me in the driver's seat, Alice in the middle, Stella in the outer passenger seat. I didn't know how intentional it was, or whose intention was at work exactly, but I was grateful for it, that I didn't have to reach between Stella's legs whenever I changed gears. And Alice didn't make a comedy out of it this time. It was just a momentary discomfort we adjusted for.

"Let's go to the lake when we get back," Alice suggested to Stella.

"Okay," said Stella. "Emily, do you want to?"

"Sure," I said. Wanting or not wanting to, as categories, didn't seem to matter in this instance. It was what I would be doing.

"Great!" said Alice, with an enthusiasm that almost passed for sincerity. Almost.

We split up to get our swimsuits and towels and I paused, considered my options, decided on a black two-piece and an old blue oxford shirt of David's as a cover-up. Stella and Alice weren't at the lake when I got there, and when they showed up, if they showed up, they'd find a blue shirt crumpled in the sand along with a bikini top. I swam out, out, out. To the darkest, coolest part of the lake, and when the water rippled in the depths beneath me, I kept still, I minded nothing, I floated.

I didn't immediately hear Alice calling me, standing on the green aluminum dock, like a bar of light in her white one-piece. Her hair a wet rope down her back. When I reached her and climbed up, I could see Stella, lying on the beach, sunbathing, and Alice was now doing her best not to look at me, at my almost naked body.

It wasn't retribution, this reversal of our first meeting. But Alice spoke first and when she did, she deferred. Thanking me for letting her be here, with Stella.

You're welcome? My pleasure? Neither of those statements seemed true. "Sure," I said. We lay down against the hot metal sheeting, eyes closed, wordless, until after a while, there was Alice's voice again.

"Stella thinks you're great."

"She does?" I wondered if I sounded too flattered, too pleased.

"Yeah. And she doesn't like everyone, you know."

"I know. I like that about her."

"I don't know you as well as she does, obviously, but I've been thinking and I really don't think you should take that job."

"Well, it's not mine to take. They haven't made an offer."

"Yeah, but they will. And I think you'd be better off embracing this mistress-of-the-manor, lady-of-leisure thing you've got going on."

"Even if I could, that's not what this is."

"No?"

"I don't know. You're the one working on theories about labor and leisure and love, so maybe you're right."

"Oh, I just say that when people ask, but I don't really know what I'm working on."

You're working on yourself, Alice. That careless, cunning, beautiful thing.

"You've got time, I guess, to figure it out."

"Sometimes it seems that way to me, but sometimes I can already feel it slipping past me. Time, I mean. Life."

I couldn't help it, I laughed. *In your wet white bathing suit, nothing has slipped past you. Not yet.*

"I was being serious."

"I know."

I'm giving you a lesson, Alice. You don't know it, and you won't get it for a while, but that's what I'm doing. Female education.

I stood up and dived off the dock, leaving Alice behind, swimming straight back to shore, and when I reached the sand, where Stella was sitting a few feet away on a towel, reading a book, I bent over to shake out my hair and then looked up to see her eyes, meeting mine. A look both frank and deciphering—it illuminated a door you didn't see before and still the door had yet to be opened. Not unlike a look I remembered from so many summers ago, at the film foundation. When I was wearing Nick's T-shirt with nothing on underneath, and his girlfriend, with the sooty hair and the long black tank top, was talking about Fassbinder, and he looked at me like he was arriving at something just out of reach.

I returned her gaze until it became something of a challenge: who would look away first. Stella did. And there was something defeated in it—*you win*—that gave me no satisfaction. That made me feel a little monstrous, even. *Get a hold of yourself, Emily. Dial it down.* I put my shirt on—David's shirt—and sat on my towel next to her.

"I feel like I'm supposed to say something about the other night," I said. "When I kissed you. But I'm not sure what I'm supposed to say."

"You don't have to say anything. I was there. I kissed you, too."

"But it upset you."

Stella looked toward the water, where Alice swam.

"I don't know if *upset* is right. I just didn't know what to do with it."

"Did you go home after and text Alice?"

"No. Yes. I mean, I did, but we'd already been texting again."

She didn't ask me what I did after and I didn't tell her, how I politely waited for Liz and Felix to leave, how red my mouth was, how I kissed David with it, kissed him until we forgot who was who.

"Are you and Alice back together?"

"I don't know what we are. But she's here. You know?" Stella had been making channels again in the sand with her heels but she stopped. A sense of defeat seemed to come over her a second time, she shrank into herself, and I wanted to do what I could to relieve her of it.

"Oh, Alice is definitely here," I said.

"It's a fact." She looked up and met my smile.

"More than a fact. She's like a universal truth. But of what, I'm not sure."

As if on cue, Alice emerged from the water, wrung out the coil of her hair, and walked up the beach toward us like she'd walk right past us before she stopped, standing over Stella.

"You're coming with me," she said.

"Where?" Stella asked.

Alice pointed to a beached canoe. Stella didn't say no. They went to the boathouse for paddles, dragged the canoe into the water, and, Alice in the bow seat, Stella at the stern, they glided out to a point where I could no longer see them. To the crop circle island, maybe. The convenience store by the other side of the lake. I imagined Alice walking across the tar parking lot and heading inside, dripping wet in her white suit, barefoot, and the young man by the cash register not even asking her what she wants. He hands over everything.

Or maybe they were just floating out there, beyond my view, in a tangle of lily pads, Alice turned to face Stella. What was the look they would give each other? Alice slowly edging over the canoe's ribs toward Stella until they're no longer looking at each other, at least not eye to eye.

I walked home, a little dazed. In my bikini bottom and David's shirt, my skin taut, as if pulled by the water as it dried. I headed straight for the desk with the computer—still no word from Samira—and did something I'd never done before. I searched for Nick, who'd given me his shirt all those years ago. I didn't remember his last name but I put what remained of my journalism skills to use and got a hit that brought it back. I'd never really wanted to know, until now, where he was or what he was doing—I wanted to keep us in that room with industrial carpeting and the chugging air-conditioning unit in the old windows, me in his shirt with nothing underneath. He no longer lived in Boston. He'd moved to Los Angeles, some time ago, it seemed. In the pictures that came up now, he was still wearing black. The woman with him in a couple of photos wasn't the woman I remembered. I didn't expect her to be, all these years later. But this woman in the pictures online had eyes like Anne Frank. Something did happen that hot afternoon when nothing happened between us.

I proceeded to look up the film foundation. It was no longer around. Or it was, but in a different form. From what I could tell, when they ran out of funding for their operating costs, the staff were absorbed into a university as a kind of satellite program for continuing education, youth mentorship, and coordination of an annual film festival. I didn't recognize the names of any of the current staff, except for the executive director. I wrote to her. I wasn't expecting a response. I was beaming a message into outer space.

RESPONSIBLE ADULTS

I showered and fell asleep, and when David gently woke me up I had no idea what time it was. But there was still a little light through the window, so it must have been evening. Late dusk.

"You're here," I said, as if I'd been wishing for him. As if, just when I'd stopped thinking it would happen, he'd shown up.

"How long have you been out?" he asked.

"A few hours. Did you just get home?"

Yes, he said. He was late because of the time-sensitive project. He'd eaten dinner at the office. He asked if I felt all right. Just sort of sun-struck, I answered. And then, as it came back to me, I told him about the day. I started with the shrubbery, naked Alice, how I took the truck out and we went for Thai food—me, Stella, Alice, and Alice's breasts—and then we all went down to the lake. I left out many things: the stick-shift sex sounds, the Puritan bitch, the graffito, my dive off the dock, Stella's lowered eyes, his blue oxford cloth shirt.

"So, Alice is here now? Alice and her breasts?"

"Just for a few days. Is that . . ." and I didn't finish the question.

"I don't know. I don't know much about her except for what Stella told me during the storm. Are we starting a home for wayward girls now?"

David wasn't stoic, he wasn't a martyr, wasn't uncomplaining. But we would have been lost without his equanimity. And sometimes I forgot that though his equanimity was deep, it was not boundless. I did the dishes so he wouldn't resent me but I hadn't done enough dishes—there weren't enough dishes to offset the weight of all these women: me, Stella, Liz, and now Alice.

"You may not even run into her," I said.

"Are they back together?" he asked.

"Unclear."

"She sounds like bad news," he said, and *bad news* had the same shifting effect as his *fuck no.* The air changed and it reconfigured us. We were no longer facing each other; at that moment we were facing in the same direction, together, examining something or someone else.

We talked about Stella and Alice in retrospective tones. As if we remembered that kind of bad news in our own lives but had put it behind us. As if Alice could interest us, in an almost clinical way, but she wouldn't obsess us, as she might have if we were Stella's age.

"Do you think you were ever bad news for someone?" I asked.

"No," he said quickly. And then slowly: "But maybe I was, and if I don't even know it, that makes me the worst news."

I found it hard to believe he would have been such bad news that he wouldn't even have known it, and at the same time, he used to say he was glad he met me when he did. That I wouldn't have liked him much before then and he wouldn't have liked me. Not in the necessary way. I knew what he meant and I knew that he was right, even as I said that I would never have not liked him.

A faint smell of wood smoke filtered through our bedroom window, which was unusual. There were only so many places it could have been coming from but the likeliest was the stone fire pit not too far from the rec hall. David and I had never used it since moving to Alder, but when I was a counselor, we would occasionally light it up on nights when a nearby boys' camp came to visit for a dance.

Neither of us particularly wanted to leave our room but the responsible thing to do was to go check it out. And we were responsible. We were adults. Were we not?

Against a distant backdrop of black trees, just before it all went dark, we saw them out there, the mercurial goddess of curves and cascading hair, and the swift, pure-hearted goddess whose hair was a dark flame, standing over their strong, steady fire, and I was relieved to note that they were both dressed.

"Hey, hey!" Alice yelled when she noticed us approaching.

Once there, David introduced himself and complimented their handiwork.

"I hope you don't mind," said Stella. "We just had the idea."

"You mean *I* had the idea," said Alice, who I assumed was annoyed with Stella's continued docility toward me. "I dragged Stella into it. I tempted her with visions of a campfire and then I convinced her to bike to the convenience store to get us these marshmallows. And matches. It's all on me. I'm an evil witch."

"Can I have one?" I asked, pointing to the bag of marshmallows, feeling my hunger, remembering that I hadn't really had dinner.

"Take this," said Alice, handing me the stick she'd been turning over. The marshmallow was perfectly browned, a little crispy outside, and completely gooey at the center.

"You *are* an evil witch," I said. "I want to eat this whole bag."

Alice stabbed another marshmallow and moved her stick over the fire as if she were conducting—which, in a sense, she was. When it was done, she gave it to David. I watched her watch him eat it, and when a sticky white speck remained on his lower lip, she ran her tongue along her own lip to point it out to him—*Lick me. Like me*—and David wiped it away with the back of his hand.

We'd all been standing, not getting settled enough to extend the moment, but there were large, flat rocks in a formation around the fire pit, and Alice and Stella sat, not going anywhere. To my surprise, David sat, too. So I followed suit.

We formed a circle: Alice, Stella, me, David. And Alice, who was not only wearing a shirt but a shirt with a pocket, pulled out a joint. She lit it and then offered it to Stella, who then didn't seem to know whether she should pass it back to Alice or give it to me. She chose me. She was simply keeping things moving clockwise in the act of sharing, but irritation flickered across Alice's face, visibly enough for me to see.

The chumminess between David and Stella was damped down, and that must have had to do with Alice's presence. I could be the recessive suburban wife, enough so that David and Stella could be the carousing husbands. But Alice would never be that recessive, that suburban, and even if she married one day, she would never be a wife.

"Alice, you're from Brooklyn Heights?" David asked, as I passed the joint along to him.

"Yup," she said, prepared to be bored by this line of conversation. And then, "Wait, how do you know that?"

"I told them," said Stella.

"You've been talking about me." Her mouth curled into a smile and she tilted her head toward Stella in a manner that wasn't entirely sweet. "And you"—she turned to David—"have been listening." Their eyes locked. Alice wasn't coy about anything. There was a ferocity to her, something unsoothed. David met it with a kind of evenness, a way of interacting he probably employed with difficult clients at work, a side of him I didn't see much of. It wasn't false, but it wasn't ours. It belonged, at the moment, to him and Alice. *I'm listening, I care about your concerns, but only because I'm getting something out of this, too.*

"You may have come up once or twice," Stella said, breaking in.

"Wow," said Alice. "You guys have become, like, this little group that I have to, like, infiltrate."

Alice looked to David again while Stella stared into the fire. And David returned her stare, reoriented himself toward her: "I'm pretty sure you could infiltrate anything you wanted to."

Alice scoffed a little because she could, because she knew she held his interest. And at the same time, she pressed herself closer to him. Their knees touched. I didn't know what to do with the prickling panic I felt. Other than what I so often did: detachment through close attention. I observed.

"Anything I want?" she said.

"I mean, you seem really capable," he added, regaining his evenness, allowing me to regain mine, passing her the joint. "You have drugs."

"I have drugs."

"And you built this fire."

"Right. Well, I am a city girl but my family also has a place up the Hudson, a country house, sort of."

We could envision it: sloping land and a pond, a rambling old manse of rough-hewn floorboards, somewhat shabbily furnished, but up-to-code electric, HVAC, and plumbing, top-of-the-line appliances in the renovated kitchen. A place where learning how to build a fire was a luxury, not at all a necessity.

"I love it there. We don't shut it up when we leave, or put sheets over furniture, that kind of thing, but there's something, like, shrouded about it." She wasn't speaking specifically to David now, more to the air, or even, more to me. "I feel like all of my secrets are there, all the good ones anyway, waiting for me, and whenever I go back it's like, *Oh, hello, you.*"

Alice. My heart instantly thawed. *Hello, you.*

"Normally, I'd be there right around now. But—"

She turned her face toward Stella again, her knee no longer touching David's, and she and Stella exchanged a slow, forgiving look that took in what had passed only between them. It said: *I'm glad you're here and nowhere else.* Another reconfiguring took place. There was no longer any little group Alice needed to infiltrate. For Alice, there was only Stella and these two middle-aged strangers hogging her marshmallows and weed.

David saw it, I saw it, and though I didn't want to leave—I wanted more of the Alice I'd glimpsed, more of the Stella who knew her—we stood again and neither of them tried to persuade us to stay.

"We should get going," said David. "Nice to meet you, Alice."

"You, too, David. And don't worry," she said, pointing to the fire. "I know how to put it out."

We walked home without looking back, in a silence that contained so much: David flirting with Alice, me saying nothing about it because I had no right, because what had I been doing with Stella? And then, look where it had taken both of us: shut out, brought to heel by these wayward girls, by their banality, their mystery. We should take hold of the situation and turn it around, ask them to leave. Tell them to. Didn't we have that power?

"We can be responsible adults," I said, and I couldn't quite tell in the dark if David nodded his head.

"Even if we can, I'm not all that sure it matters," he said.

"We can tell them we're done, that we're sorry but they have to go. Not even that we're sorry."

"Yeah."

Another silence, one in which I heard only our footsteps and the soft, surging hum of crickets. I could sense him thinking.

"What is it?"

"I think we're the ones that need to go."

I wanted to be able to agree. To accept that the time had come. But all I felt was a seizing in my chest. *No. Not yet.*

"You know, my first real job site was in Brooklyn Heights," he said. "Converting a cut-up brownstone back into a single-family home. The family that was going to live there had a lot of demands and a young daughter who also had some very specific ideas. I highly doubt it was Alice's family, that's not where I'm going with this. But when I was working there, I'd walk on the Promenade and wonder about this child I was more or less working for. Like she'd already figured out, even at that age, how everything worked, who was in charge and in control, and I was only slowly catching on. How can I still only be catching on?"

"Do you know the *one thing* I'm in complete control of?" I said.

He laughed a little and said *no* at the same time. A no-laugh.

"Our TV remote."

"That's not funny," he said, but he gave another laugh.

"But control is really such a weird thing. Because it shifts, it changes. Who is in control, and control over what? What does *control* even mean?" I'd become Alice for a moment, arguing at a theoretical remove.

"That makes control sound like a matter of semantics, and it's more than that. You don't feel that it's more than that?" No more laughing, just a note of rising irritation.

"No, I know it's more than that," I said. I could still smell the fire in the air, though it was out of sight now, behind trees. We were crossing the field by the basketball court, a flat expanse that was so regular and intelligible, so known during the day, but was astonishing, almost dizzying in the darkness. Though I knew exactly where we were walking, the contours of the world seemed to disappear.

"You can't just endlessly reframe things," he said, a voice in the formlessness.

"No, but don't you think perspective matters?"

"Maybe," said David. "Maybe you can change your perspective to give yourself some sense of agency, but there's a difference between that and actually having control." He'd stopped moving and he'd reached out for my arm. "There are actual, lasting consequences that happen as a result of who has control and who doesn't, and those consequences matter."

"Of course there are consequences that matter," I said. I didn't pull away, even as my own irritation surfaced. Irritation and something else, something more elemental, more powerful. "I get that there are things that can't be controlled and can't be reframed. Things you can't change no matter how hard you try. You don't think I get that?" I couldn't see his face, only the outline of him. "I get it so *fucking* clearly. Sometimes it's the *only* thing I fucking get."

He couldn't see my face, only my outline, but he could hear me start to cry and he drew me in, so that I could sob into his shoulder. I cried so hard I shook and he held me until I stopped. He moved my wet hair out of my face, brushed it back, kissed me, on my mouth, off to the side, on my cheekbone, my forehead.

We were so sad, so damp from our sadness, walking back to our house. Once inside, though, it was as if what happened out there in the night was meant to stay out there and not in these lighted rooms.

We went to the kitchen and ate whatever we could pull out of the fridge or cupboards and didn't have to do anything to, items we could simply put into our mouths. Unthinking consumption of one kind and then another: we lay on the couch, my legs across his, and I pressed play, and we didn't have to talk or make decisions or consider what was out of our control. All we had to do was watch what was in front of us onscreen. And David didn't even have to do that—he fell asleep before too long and when I pressed pause, got up to wake him, he mumbled something, extended himself along the length of the couch, and fell back asleep.

I placed a blanket over him—*I would never have not liked you*—and headed upstairs, where I'd left my phone, where there was a missed call, from earlier that day, and a follow-up email from Samira: It was great to meet me. Would I be interested in coming in for a second conversation? She hoped so and she was very much looking forward to it. Once again, as it had those first days with Stella, time had slowed and warped. It hadn't been very long, no more than a week, though meeting with Samira now felt like a distant memory.

From a window in the room at the end of the hall, the room where Stella found Aunt Esther's robe, I could see out across the field to where the fire pit was. But there wasn't much to see now. The flames were gone and I could barely make out the black trees.

MADAME X

A pale sky, a cool morning. David didn't ask why I wanted to go with him to Boston, he simply accepted it, approving. We parked by the commuter rail and rode in together, not talking, but not not-talking, the quiet tethering us together, until we let it go at South Station. He headed to his office and I took the T to the Back Bay Fens, where all the green of August had grown tired of being green. No one had any more energy to pull weeds or rake the dusty paths that wound through the park. I followed the trails, over ironwork bridges and under leafy canopies, and ended up, without really intending to, at the Venetian palace that Isabella Stewart Gardner built to house her late-nineteenth-century art collection. On school field trips, we'd learned about this extraordinarily wealthy, adventurous woman from a corseted era of excess, her travels and her jewels, her dashing flamboyance. We learned about her as we learned about the pilgrims and the *Mayflower* in Plymouth. Massachusetts lore. I remembered the museum's glass-roofed, flowering courtyard but I hadn't come here often enough to recall a small interior room where the walls were covered in blue silk and there hung a painting, *Madame Gautreau Drinking a Toast*, by John Singer Sargent.

A young woman with dark, upswept hair, pale skin, sitting at a brown tabletop, pale pink flowers surrounding the glass in her hand. She wears a black dress that exposes her arms, which are covered by a diaphanous blush wrap. You don't see who she's holding her glass toward, and her expression, in profile, suggests indifference. Not unlike the expression she would wear a year later when Sargent painted her in full, in another low-cut black dress, her arms and shoulders bare, the scandalous *Madame X*. She didn't remind me, at first, of any woman in particular, more like every woman I've known, at some point in their lives that bored and that beautiful. But then, in particular, Liz came to mind. The particular boredom of Liz. Boredom that spoke not of a lack of imagination, but of what happens when imagination is too keen for its context, when it meets no match.

She couldn't get lunch, Liz told me when I called her from outside the museum. But she could manage a late coffee someplace near the campus building where she was handling some administrative work before she resumed teaching a class in the fall. It wasn't too far for me to walk and all I had was time.

When she saw me she seemed both delighted and distracted.

"We need to do this more often," she said. "What's wrong with us?"

"Probably depends who you ask," I said. But maybe this would become more frequent, meeting up in the day, if or when I would be working in the city. I told her about the second interview I'd scheduled with Samira at the end of the week. That's really great, Liz said. She didn't qualify it this time.

She did ask about Stella and I told her Stella was still on our property, in the bunk, but that there wasn't much else to report. I didn't mention Alice. There was something satisfying in simply omitting her.

I hadn't consciously planned this city excursion as a means of staying out of their path, Stella and Alice. I hadn't wanted my actions to merely be a reaction to them. But it served that purpose. A day away from them, from the lake, from the bunks, the camp. From the positions we'd put ourselves in. All of it.

I asked Liz about her classes that semester.

"What are your students like?"

"They're young," she said. *Like Stella. Like Alice.* Her wistfulness softened the harshness of both the envy and the superiority in her tone. "I'm supposed to say I love teaching because it keeps me fresh. Keeps me literally on my toes. And it does. I'm not trying to be all hardened and surly or like I'm only in it for the money when there's barely any money. I wouldn't do it if it wasn't rewarding—on some level. I do get something out of it and I'd like to think that my students get something out of it. But, yeah, they're so young. And what I mean is that they don't get the irony of it, the depressing paradox of dancing—that by the time you have the emotional breadth and depth to fully express what you want to, you no longer have the body for it. Your knee hurts or you've twisted your ankle too many times. And you shouldn't get the irony of it—I never got it when I was that age—not getting it is what gives you power, as a dancer. You're *in* it, you know? You're not sure of yourself because you haven't had enough experience, which is different than the kind of doubt that comes with too much experience. You're not thinking about it, overanalyzing it. So I think what I really mean is, getting the irony, being old enough to get the irony, isn't much of a consolation. It just makes me angry and frustrated when it doesn't make me resigned."

"You make irony sound like a disease."

"I have irony."

"It's a chronic condition."

Liz: That broad smile of hers that compressed time as it expanded it. I forgot for a minute where we were, who we were. *When* we were. But it was impossible to sustain. Even if she didn't have to go, to pick up her kids, the minute would have passed there at the café table. Time doesn't suspend itself.

And it was normalizing to be in the flow of it. David was working late again so I took the train back on my own but at an hour when the platform and the car were full of people do-ing the same. Nobody looked at me like I didn't belong there,

nobody looked at me much at all, and being an indistinguish-
able part of a crowd was a relief, an intimation of what it would
be like to do this every day, to have a commute, to seamlessly
occupy some recognizable, approved-of role in society. It
would get old, it had already gotten old for David, I knew,
but that evening, for me, it was a comfort. And approaching it
from that angle, even our house had a different cast to it. Not
so removed from the world. Not a place to leave but a place to
come home to.

Changing out of the day's clothes, into a worn shirt and
soft, forgiving shorts, the kind sold as pajamas, I thought about
the women in housecoats. Maybe they hadn't entirely disappeared, they'd only morphed, *we'd* only morphed, into a new
incarnation. And as I was thinking this, standing by the bay
window in the living room, the one that had no covering, I saw
Alice through the glass, crossing into the yard. She looked up
and stared at me, as I'd stared at the elderly woman with the
bright lipstick in the housecoat in the dun-colored suburb as we
drove away from a city along highways until we arrived here.

I hadn't thought, at the time, about what she was seeing,
the woman in the housecoat. Or rather, it had seemed to me
that she wasn't seeing. That, in standing in the window in such
a way, she was more interested in being seen. But that had been
a failure of my imagination, to not grasp the whole of it, only
my part.

Alice stared at me, a little taken aback, it seemed—she
was on her way here but hadn't expected to catch me in the
window—and I stared at her, in her strappy white sundress

that she filled so well, her soft arms and shoulders exposed like Madame Gautreau. Her hair in a falling-out braid, her face flushed from walking. She waved and then pointed, indicating she wanted to go around and meet at the door.

I did as she wanted, not reluctantly, but not enthusiastically either. I was a little tired, of the situation. I was like all the green in the park I'd walked through that morning. And I had a chronic condition.

"Hi," she said.

We stood there for a moment, as if reenacting our time at the window.

"I kind of feel like a vampire," she said. "Waiting for you to invite me in so I can cross the threshold."

"Oh. Yeah, come in."

"I just thought I'd see if you were around. Stella's at work and I'm kind of bored. And hungry."

If she were Stella, I would have already ushered her into the kitchen and we wouldn't have been standing in the hall-way. And I thought: *Why this person and not that one?* David would have said it had to do with timing. Meaning not only coincidence or the alignment of certain circumstances, but where each of you is within time. *You wouldn't have liked me then and I wouldn't have liked you.* What if it had been Alice I'd found in bunk 18? If I'd removed Alice's splinter and let her stay? But it wouldn't have been Alice.

"David's at work, too," I said, to find and center our commonality. "I was going to have some wine and make a pizza." And then, as if it were an obligation, like a meal David and

I would have provided for our lodgers, I asked if she wanted to join me. Clearly she did and I wasn't sure why but I didn't want to disappoint her. Alice and her good secrets.

"I knew you guys would have a pizza stone and all the fixings," she said. It sounded a little like an indictment. We were those kind of people. Even though she was, too.

"I was thinking frozen pizza," I said. "But, yes, we do have a stone. And fixings."

"My lucky night," she said. "Your lucky night, actually. I'll make it for us."

And though I wanted to rewind, go back a bit and tell her I was worn out from the day, that she was welcome to grab some food but I wasn't up for company, she was already checking the oven, opening cupboard doors, finding what she needed, uncorking a bottle of red and pouring us each a glass. She was so at home in a house that wasn't hers that I didn't feel dispossessed of something that was mine; I only wondered, in a half-thinking way, what possession even was. I was drinking her wine. I would eat her food.

I helped her find what she needed, ingredients and utensils, working under her direction. But mostly I finished what was in my glass and refilled it, as if this were my true vocation.

"I'm worried about your white dress," I said. "And this wine and this tomato sauce."

"I could take it off," she said. Apparently, we had already reached the point where we had a past and could joke about it, joke about our respective nakedness in it.

"I was thinking I could get you an apron."

"Ah. Sure. Okay."

When she put it on—plain, dark blue canvas—she looked even more at home, but not necessarily in a domestic way; she took on the air of an artist in the studio. If something bothered me about Alice, it wasn't her entitlement. Her entitlement justified itself because it was so bound up with capability. She seemed entitled to everything because she was capable of anything. And I knew that was an exaggeration, but it was the thought that came.

"How was your day?" she asked, taking care of getting conversation going.

"It was nice." I told her I went to Boston, to a park, to a museum, saw a friend for coffee. I left out the part about time compressing and expanding. "What were you up to today?"

"Oh, you know, taking it easy, mostly. Stella and I hung out a bunch and then she left for her shift. I read for a while. Gave myself a mani-pedi." And that's when I noticed her crimson nails. How could I not have noticed before, when she was using the corkscrew or rolling out the dough? It was as though her nails had had no color on them and now, just like that, they did.

"You didn't use the blue," I said.

"No, that's Stella's color. The crimson is more me."

I almost couldn't bring myself to look at my own hands, as if they were betraying me with their chipped red polish. It didn't even look like the same shade, and I didn't want to ascribe too much meaning to Stella telling me it was my color and Alice now telling me it was hers. It was time, more than time, for me to remove it completely.

"It does look nice on you," I said.

"Thank you."

She closed her hand around a ball of mozzarella, with no apparent drama or premeditation, but I experienced it as if watching a movie, like an iris shot, blackness encircling and closing in on that detail in the frame.

"When do you go back to school?" I asked.

"Can't wait to get rid of me?"

"No, I was just having that coming-of-fall feeling today, you know what I mean? The end of summer, when everything starts looking tired."

"Yeah. Seasons."

I laughed and she turned to me, questioning.

"You have this way of laughing at things I say when I don't mean them to be funny," she said.

"I'm sorry. I don't mean to. It's just, something about *yeah, seasons*. It seemed kind of profound and ridiculous at the same time."

Alice thought for a moment.

"Well, at this point, seasons are more of a marketing concept than anything. You know, like, it's time for a fall wardrobe refresh! Sweater weather! Isn't that the kind of campaign you'll be doing for that online shop?"

"I guess. If I get that job. But, atmospherically, don't you still feel something aside from what you're commercially bombarded with? I mean, the light still changes in certain months. The air changes. The mood changes."

"Sure, but it still seems kind of arbitrary. Depending on

where you live. And it's only getting more arbitrary. Are we even gonna *have* seasons in twenty years? In ten years?"

"Right. What will the marketers do?"

"Oh, they'll get a new concept. Someone's going to profit from all of it. Someone always does."

If cynicism was a comfort of the powerless, a release valve for pent-up rage, then what Alice was expressing was not cynicism but something else. Some knowingness bound up with confidence—perhaps derived from her parents, from Brooklyn Heights, from Harvard—that there was, that there always would be, a place for her. My brother had gone to Harvard, and I remembered how the tone of his college graduation was largely one of optimism and triumph: *Here we are, world.* The tone at my not-Harvard graduation was different, a measure of some accomplishment cut with searching anxiety: *Okay, so now what?*

As she talked, Alice put the pizza in the oven and assessed the preparatory mess with an exacting analytical quickness so at odds with her blowzy, loose physicality. In an orderly, efficient fashion, she began cleaning up. As if, again, it were not my house, as if I were the guest here, I offered to help and she said, no, no, no, sit, drink. But dishes filled the sink now and doing dishes was my specialty. I knew what to do with dishes, what to do with myself when I was doing dishes, so I started rinsing, getting into enough of a rhythm that when my hair fell into my face, I didn't want to stop to fix it.

"Here," Alice said, coming up, not quite against me but

so close that we were almost touching. She must have been watching me, attentive enough to notice the hair falling over my eyes, which she pushed away, her fingers along my temple, my ear, my neck.

"Thank you."

She stayed right as she was, long enough to force me, so that I had no choice but to turn to her. She took the sponge from my hand and placed it on the counter, a setting-in-motion gesture. If I had put my free, damp hand on her back, her shoulder, out of some momentary, instinctive propulsion, what would she have done? Instead I simply stood there, near motionless and confused, and she turned that curling, not-nice smile on me, the smile she gave Stella by the fire last night.

"You're not going to kiss me, too?" she said.

She'd done what she must have come here this evening to do. To make clear to me that if Stella was not hers, she was also not mine. If Stella were mine, at all, in any way that mattered, she wouldn't have told Alice about what happened after the dinner party on the infirmary steps. She wouldn't have shared what was between us with this young woman whose voraciousness hadn't yet found a focus, whose voraciousness was let loose without one clear target and hit me because I happened to be in the way. Because I'd put myself in the way.

I backed away from her. My face was burning, from this and the wine, but still I could feel the color, the blood, draining.

"I'm sorry." Her wicked smile dissolved. "It was just the moment," she said. "I didn't mean to overstep."

"Yes, you did," I managed. "You did mean it."

She sighed, with an air of exasperation and boredom. It was maddening.

"Fine. So what if I did?"

"You've totally crossed the line."

"Oh, *now* all of a sudden there's a line?"

"Yes, there's a fucking line!"

"Seems to me like it keeps moving. Like you keep moving it to suit yourself."

"What do you want, Alice? Just tell me." It came out more pleading than I would have liked.

"I want to know something. I want to know how it is you get to walk around here like a queen and an invalid. Like you rule over everyone while they wait on you and take care of you. How does that happen?"

"You've been here, what, a few days, and you already know all about me?"

"Pretty much."

"Is this for your research? Into women and leisure and love or whatever?"

"I think it's for my fucking life. I just don't know if you're, like, my role model or a total cautionary tale."

If I teared up, which is what I could feel happening, then I was only making Alice's point for her.

"I'll be both," I said. "You can have it both ways. Okay?"

"I'm not trying to be a bitch," she offered.

I was sitting down in a kitchen chair now, I realized, looking up at her. She was a little blurry in her white dress with her red nails and her hair had a golden, fuzzy aura around it.

"You sure about that?"

"I just wanted to clear the air."

"Right," I said. I stared into the floor, took a breath, looked up. "Well, in the spirit of clearing the air, you can't stay here any longer."

"That's fine," she replied, infuriatingly unflappable. "I wasn't planning on being here much longer anyway."

"I mean you have to leave tonight."

And that was enough to provoke an incredulous, petulant sound from her throat.

"What am I supposed to tell Stella?"

I summoned composure from who knows where. Getting up to turn off the faucet, which had been running this whole time, I resumed the dishes, my back to Alice. "Tell her whatever you want. You'll figure something out."

But Alice wasn't done. "Who do you think Stella is?" she said.

What did she mean? Was she going to tell me something awful about Stella? I turned to face her.

"Who do you think *you* are?" she added, hands on her hips, assessing me as she might a piece of art she didn't particularly care for. "What do you want with her?"

I couldn't answer. I could only look away, focus on

everything in the sink, and continue scrubbing, as if the motions were keeping me together, and only together enough to say: "You can go now, Alice." Half queen, half invalid.

I didn't see her out, I didn't watch her leave, she didn't slam doors, she disappeared and I cleared the sink, and then I sat down, shaking. The oven timer dinged and though I thought I had no appetite, I ate the whole pizza in one sitting. I finished the bottle of wine, too.

END OF THE SEASON

I should have saved half of the pizza for David, but Alice had made me ungenerous, thoughtless—really, I couldn't think—and all I could do was devour whatever was in front of me. That's what I would have said when David came through the door. But he texted me instead, telling me not to wait up, so I watched another movie, sedated by the wine, and was asleep in our room by the time he got home. I murmured a few barely awake words to him when he got in bed, and when his alarm clock sounded in the morning, I woke apprehensive and went down to the kitchen, furtive, before David did, as though I expected to see something I'd forgotten to hide.

But there was no trace of what had happened with Alice. And why should it have been incriminating anyway? What had I done wrong? I wasn't sure anymore.

"I asked Alice to leave last night," I said to David when he came into the room. "I told her to."

"What happened?"

What happened—it hit me like a rough, churning wave— *was that she put me in my place. She got in my way. She made me angry. She made my heart race. She frustrated me. She touched my face and froze me. She made me so protective, so fearful of losing what I couldn't even name that I wanted to destroy something I couldn't name. So I sent her away and gorged myself on a pizza.*

"I don't know," I said. "She came by and she just made me really uncomfortable. More of the same from the other night by the fire. Just too much, you know?"

"What did Stella say?" he asked.

"Nothing, to me. She was out, at work, I think."

"So maybe they're both gone."

"Maybe."

How had this not dawned on me until now? I had envisioned a tense conversation with Stella, a sort of reckoning, but I had envisioned her still *here*. There. In the bunk, her bunk.

I kept my cool. David and I had coffee, ate breakfast—he didn't have time to see what the situation with Stella might be. His presentation, what had been keeping him late, was scheduled for later that morning and he had to get moving.

"You're going to be great," I said.

"Thanks."

"I'm really sorry," I said. "I feel like this is like one of those situations where you can't ask someone's name because you're already supposed to know it, like they've told you a number of times and you just haven't been paying attention, and that's terrible—but I don't know what this project is that you've been working on and it's seemed like it's too late for me to ask."

"Well, thanks for asking, but I guess I hadn't told you much about it because there's not much to tell, it's not all that interesting. I mean, from any perspective other than a problem-solving one."

"But you've solved the problem?"

Maybe, he said. He would have to see. He'd know more tonight. Things would ease up by the weekend, he thought, and he wouldn't be stuck at work so late.

"That would be nice. To have a night together. Just us."

"I'd like that."

I had no real reason to assume he didn't mean it. He nodded, smiled, kissed me, left.

Wait, my inner invalid-queen would have said. *Come back! Don't leave!* But strangely, it was as if that voice, detected and diagnosed by Alice, might have disappeared with her. I didn't feel the grasping urge to hold to David, to anyone, really. Only the absence of the urge. In sending Alice away, I might have solved another problem.

I checked my phone. Nothing from Stella.

I put on my housecoat-equivalent clothes—I had housekeeping, of a sort, to do—and went over to her bunk. I knocked. No answer. The solid exterior door had been left open, and the screen door in front of it was closed, but unlocked; it could only be locked from the inside with a latch and nobody was there. Alice's red sleeping bag was gone. And there was only one piece of baggage on the floor, Stella's zipped-up green duffel. The rest of Stella's belongings were still there, neatly arranged as they'd always been. Her two bottles of polish and remover, the set of jacks, on top of the dresser she'd requisitioned for herself. Aunt Esther's silk robe hanging from a nail.

I didn't have the drive to snoop through her things, though it was tempting, maybe in the way it is for a parent, merely because I had the opportunity, alone in a quiet house at an off hour, your teenager's room just down the hall. What had Robin Dart done when faced with the situation? Robin Dart, David Bowie–loving Robin Dart, would have remembered what it was like to be a particular kind of teenage girl, the kind you see in the audience of the concert footage in *Ziggy Stardust and the Spiders from Mars*—ardent, ecstatic, alive, in love not so much with an individual but with a way of being in the world embodied to the fullest by that individual at that moment. Bowie announces at the end that it's the last show he'll ever do as Ziggy Stardust, announcing the death of that moment. But the girls, and the boys, know a spectacular way of being in the world now and they'll take that with them beyond the moment, when they leave the concert hall, or when they leave their bedrooms, when, like Robin Dart, they grow up and have children of their own. When they give those children names.

Robin Dart lived in the western part of the state with a boyfriend Stella didn't like much, but aside from that, Stella

was on good, if not particularly close, terms with her mother.
She didn't need another mother. She didn't need another girlfriend. She had Alice, more or less. She needed a place to live
for a while and that is what I gave her, that's all she wanted
from me. Who did I think I was? I saw it plainly just then.

I'm sorry, I messaged her. I didn't say for what, exactly.

Hours later she replied: *It's okay*. She didn't specify what *it*
was, what was okay.

Alice was gone, Stella wasn't around but it was "okay," and
David texted to say he would be late again. Our house was
like a boat on the sea. The *Aunt Esther*. Occasionally I walked
around on deck, jumped overboard for a swim, but mostly I
stayed inside, in my quarters. There was entertainment (movies, on the couch) and there was dining (our fridge). Our house
was a cruise ship. With one passenger. I wasn't sure who the
captain was.

I watched *Je, Tu, Il, Elle* by Chantal Akerman. A young
woman, played by Akerman herself, has just moved in to an
apartment—a furnished room that she unfurnishes. She doesn't
leave for days, she handwrites letters, she undresses but doesn't
change her clothes—an oversized dark button-up shirt, thick,
comfy socks. She sleeps on a sheetless twin mattress. And she
eats powdered sugar by the spoonful from a paper bag. Once,
twice, three times, and then steadily—jabbing the spoon into

the bag and ceaselessly into her mouth. It's a repetitive, gluttonous act, a combination of compulsion and freedom, of carelessness and focused engagement. She is drifting, without going anywhere. She lies on the mattress and listens to herself breathing. She waits and waits. She looks at her reflection in the windows at night, naked. She looks straight at the camera and smiles beautifully. A half hour into the film, she finally puts on a different outfit, a kind of shiny vinyl, white-zippered jacket over a T-shirt, leaves the room, and heads out to a highway where she hitches a ride with a truck driver, for the film's second act. They go to rest-stop diners, she gives him a hand job while he talks about his family, she watches him shave in a bathroom. Or rather, we watch her watch him. Eventually, she goes to the apartment of an ex-girlfriend, presumably, and they spend one night together. She eats Nutella sandwiches and they have sex that sort of looks like two marble statues wrestling.

I'd watched this film analytically, academically, the first time I'd seen it, years ago for an undergraduate class. I'd watched it because I'd had to, because it was assigned. I'd recognized what I thought I was supposed to recognize—the attention it pays to its subject and the attention it demands of its audience. Here is a young woman, just being. But I hadn't fully comprehended how daring that was. Not simply for its time—1974—but still. For Akerman to have the confidence to think: this is worth filming, worth watching.

The character reminded me of Stella. Akerman's hair, in the black and white, was dark as ink and glossy, like Stella's.

And what did Stella do alone in the bunk, at night? Aside from play jacks. But the character reminded me more of myself now. She'd been there all along, only I hadn't recognized her.

I hadn't identified with this work in any real emotional way the first time I saw it, despite the fact that Akerman was in her early twenties when she wrote and directed it, around the age I had been then. Around Stella's age. I had been too close to it, then, maybe. I had had, on some level, this never-spoken thought: *I could do that or something like it. Make something like that.* A thought both admiring and dismissive, a thought you can have only when your own creative ambition is still coalescing but untested. When who knew what you were capable of in all the time you had ahead of you? I registered the self-belief that Akerman must have had and inwardly took it as a kind of competitive challenge. I took it for granted, that such self-belief could be sustained, that it didn't disappear one day. I needed distance for this movie to floor me, to become something whose very existence astonished me. To come to see that self-belief for the fleeting, elusive wonder that it was. I had to be alone on the living room couch, years later, in the afternoon, in Aunt Esther's house at Alder, all that time behind me.

Two days passed and I saw a little more of David but nothing of Stella. Going forward, I figured, she would stay here, quietly, out of our way, as she did before we knew she was here, and then she would leave or we would leave. A final performance was never announced, but something had ended. So where would our ardency and our ecstasy go? Where would that way of being alive in the world go?

I tried to put a little of it into a new phase that would start with the prospect of this job at Samira's company. Our second conversation was scheduled and I hadn't asked for Stella's help in choosing clothes this time. I decided on a black shirtdress, with the right amount of shape, that I'd steamed in the night and hung in the corner of my bedroom, where I'd set out everything else I'd need to go with it today at Samira's office: a notebook with my initials stamped in gilt, my heels and my flats, a bronze cuff, my mascara, my lipstick, my structured-but-not-severe leather tote. Competent adult. Stylish enough co-worker. I was double-checking my underwear situation when there was a knock on the front door that didn't stop.

It was Stella, but Stella as I'd never seen her. Anxious, jittery, pale, out of breath. Holding her phone in her palm like it was a small, stiff, dead thing she didn't know what to do with, except extend it toward me. I took it from her, though I had no idea what to do with it either. It had been off, she explained, last night, and she'd woken up to a series of short, disturbing texts from Alice and an even more distressing voice mail. I was still holding the phone but Stella was operating it, playing the voice mail on speaker, both of us leaning over the device, like surgeons over an operating table.

It's me. Please call me. I need help. Please. I'm so alone. I'm scared. I don't know what to do. Please call me. Please.

Alice's voice. But strange and small. Not Alice-like at all.

And she hadn't been responding or picking up when Stella had continually tried to reach her this morning. It was Friday. I'd sent Alice away on Tuesday night.

Did you see her leave on Tuesday night? Have you talked to her since? Has she done anything like this before?

I asked Stella questions, I'm not sure in what order, I wasn't entirely conscious of asking them, and I absorbed answers the same way.

Stella was upset with Alice when she left and wanted time apart, Alice had said things once or twice that seemed to come from a place she usually kept well-hidden. They hadn't talked but they'd texted, nothing serious, though.

"Do you know where she is?" I asked.

"No. Her apartment? But she could be anywhere. What do I do?"

"Do you know her neighbors? Or the super for her building?"

"Not really. No."

"All right. We'll go, together, and find her, check on her. I've got the car today, I have this interview, so we'll drive to Cambridge, wherever Alice lives, and we'll start there."

"You have another interview—"

"It's not 'til later. It'll be fine. Or we'll figure it out."

I gathered up everything I had set out and we took off.

Stella, I kept assuring her on the road, try not to worry, though my own insides were turning to lead. The highway drive was quick, uneventful, but the red lights on local roads were excruciating. Still, we got there in under an hour. A brick apartment building on a tree-lined street. Stella knew the code for the lobby doors and I tried to keep pace as she took the stairs in twos to the third floor, where Alice lived. She hit the buzzer, she knocked hard.

Hold on, we heard. An unhurried, male voice on the other side. The lock turning with no real urgency.

"Hey, what's up," he said. Not because he knew or recognized either of us but because, I sensed, this was how he greeted the world. Even when the world was banging frantically at the door. An easygoing, confident, young white man. In boxer briefs.

"Is Alice here?" Stella asked.

"Yeah. Alice. She's in the shower."

"Is she okay?"

"Yeah? She's fine. I mean, why wouldn't she be?"

Stella stared at him.

"I mean, I don't know. You want to see for yourselves?"

"Who are you?" Stella asked.

"I'm Brian."

"Okay. Brian—" Stella stopped, at a loss for what to say.

"Why don't you guys come in. She'll be out in a minute. I'm sure it's fine."

Brian's trusting faith in appearances. We were strangers but he didn't rate us as any kind of threat. How *did* he rate us? He was sure it was fine, all of it. We went inside, the two of us standing there with Brian in his underwear, who noticed I was winded and asked me if I'd like a glass of water. He didn't go so far as to call me "ma'am."

"No, I'm fine," I said, waving his offer away. "Thanks."
Thanks?

Stella, who knew this place, its parquet floors and plaster walls, glanced around for a clue, some sign to help her make sense of what was happening, when Alice came out of the bathroom, one towel wrapped around her body, the other around her head.

"What the fuck?" Alice said.

"What the *fuck*? Are you fucking kidding me, Alice?" said Stella.

"What are you doing here?"

"I don't know, trying to make sure you're not *dead*?"

Alice frowned. "I'm fine."

"Yeah, Brian told us. And by the way, who *are* you, Brian?"

"He's a friend," Alice answered. Fixing me with a hard look.

Brian, finally, took Alice's tone as a cue to go to the other room and get dressed.

"You can't do this," Stella cried. She didn't seem to be addressing *what* Alice was doing so much as *how* she was doing it. The injustice of her detachment.

"Stella, calm down," said Alice.

"No, you don't get to tell me that. You leave this alarming shit on my phone and then, what, you couldn't pick up *your* phone because you were too busy fucking Brian this morning?"

"I'm sorry." Her manner softened. It was as if saying the words loosened something in Alice, the part of her that truly was sorry, the part that had left that voice mail.

"I don't—I just—Jesus fucking Christ."

Now Stella was the winded one. And Alice, for the first time I'd ever seen, was abashed. She moved to stand close to Stella, trying to find some way to shape her body around Stella's stiff but trembling stance, and she spoke into the space between them in that strange, small voice again. A supplicating voice. Her bath towel opened and fell to the floor but she didn't pick it up. She didn't even notice. How many times was I going to see her naked? Only this was so different from that first encounter outside the bunk, when her nakedness had seemed like armor. Now she was a soft creature without its shell. I couldn't entirely make out what she said, but it sounded like an expression of need. *I needed you. And then I didn't want to need you. So I went out. And I'm so sorry and I hate it, I hate it.*

Stella shook her head like if she shook it hard enough she could make Alice, this situation, vanish. Then she turned and ran out into the hallway. Alice didn't move except to lift her eyes and look to me as if for help. A look of such messed-up need and pathos that I wanted to help her, safely wrap her back up in the towel. Except my loyalty lay with Stella, who I went after, following her as she rushed down the stairs, out of the lobby, onto the sidewalk. We sat on the curb and she covered her mouth with her hand, squeezed her eyes shut, and sobbed.

I put my arms around her while she cried so hard, so ceaselessly that it was as if I were rocking her. The two of us in a kind of rhythmic trance for I don't know how long, until eventually, she sniffed a little, took one rattled breath and then another. Stella, on good terms with Robin Dart, didn't need another mother. But I suppose I still needed a child.

Alice was troubled enough, wise enough, ashamed enough, worried for herself enough, *something* enough not to come down to the street. If she'd sent Brian away, he must have used a back door or hurried past as I was consoling Stella.

"Let's go," I said, helping Stella to her feet.

"I'm sorry I dragged you here for this."

"Don't be sorry."

By the clock in the car, I had an hour and a half until my meeting with Samira.

"I can cancel it, reschedule it," I said.

"No, that would be dumb," she said.

I decided to keep the appointment and in the meantime I took Stella for lunch, to a sandwich shop, where she remained quiet, in her own head, and didn't eat much. *Stay here*, I told her, instructed her, while I went to change clothes. What would I have done if she took off? She wouldn't take off. I had earned her compliance, if not her trust.

In the washroom, I was wilted and salty with my dried sweat and Stella's tears. I had done this before in a bathroom in Boston. Years ago, removing what I had on and getting into the clean shirt that belonged to Nick. This bathroom was nicer, better lit. But there I was, again, putting on a black shirt—shirtdress, more wrinkled now, not so unlike the shirt Chantal Akerman wore in the unfurnished room—and trying to muss my hair in a stylish way. Would it be good enough for

Samira, would it make her look twice, make her want me? I didn't know, but it would have to do.

"You look good," Stella said, called back to the moment, to what was in front of her, when I reappeared. "Confident."

"Thanks," I said. Still boosted by her opinion, still trusting her judgment, on this at least.

When we got to Fort Point, Stella told me she'd stay in the car.

"You'll roast in the car."

"Then I'll go to a coffee shop or something."

"No, just come up. It's like a lounge. It's nice. Sofas. Magazines. It'll be good."

She was too unfocused to argue. And maybe I was too unfocused as well. Or too focused in a certain direction, to the detriment of another. We clanged on up the steps of the old warehouse and when Jenna greeted me, her face fell, almost imperceptibly, but not quite.

"You've brought a friend!" Her chirpiness barely concealed confusion, or disapproval.

"This is my—this is Stella," I said.

"Nice to meet you," said Jenna. She shook Stella's hand and offered to get her some water or tea, if she'd like? She directed her to a sofa upholstered in a rich green velvet with chrome accents, by a low glass table with an arrangement of fresh-cut flowers. Stella sat down quietly and I knew I'd made a mistake, a tactical error. Stella—in a thin shirt you could see her black bra through and the striped shorts she'd slept in the night before, half-dressed essentially, her face still blotchy from crying—was something I never really expected she could be: out of place. And I had put her there.

Jenna walked me back to Samira's office and once again I was the elk whose attention she tried to hold, only this time I got the feeling they were having second thoughts about elk. They had been planning to give an elk a chance but now they'd realized they needed a wilier, quicker creature in this role.

The conversation with Samira went well, though. She really did seem happy to see me again. We talked in more detail about the work, the scope of the position, about salary in terms that were agreeable if still vague. I pitched a few ideas to her, ways I might do things, strategies I had, and she was more than receptive. It was so easy to fall into cliché, she said, and she loved that I wasn't bringing tired thinking to this, that I wasn't afraid to be a little out there. I wasn't sure what she meant by "out there" but I went with it, and she was so effusive and encouraging I almost forgot to be distracted. But when she walked me to the front, when I awkwardly introduced her to Stella, a light went out, some brightness in her extinguished itself. Samira had a son—Raf, she called him. Kindergarten age. She'd mentioned him a couple of times and there were pictures on her desk: curly hair, dark, liquid eyes. She understood the challenge of balancing work and family. That sometimes there was no balance, only spillage, and that that was life in late capitalist America. But she didn't understand what this—Stella on the sofa—was. I didn't understand what this was. The closest I can come to describing it is that I'd brought my child to the office before I'd even gotten the job, before I'd even had a child.

•

We leaned against a railing by the channel, gray-brown water below, a deep blue, cloudless sky above, the old mercantile buildings, the narrow streets at our backs. Two women you would see in a photograph, dark hair lifted and blown a little in the breeze, one younger, one older, and wonder what they were to each other, how they came to be standing there in exhaustion and some release.

But I'm making us into an image, a suspended moment, and we couldn't be that. I wasn't sure what we could be, out in the world, away from the seclusion of camp. Samira and Jenna were up there in their loft office looking at each other like: *What the fuck was that?* Samira was crossing me off her list, irritated that she still had to fill this job, but relieved, too. *Dodged that bullet*, Jenna would say. *Guess it's back to the drawing board?* And Samira would agree, despite being a little crestfallen by Jenna's reliance on conversational clichés. *Maybe . . . ?* Samira, second-guessing the situation, reminding herself of my not-tired ideas . . . *maybe . . . no. Just no.*

I saw us through a Samira-Jenna lens: Stella and I met online, we're into role playing, some kind of aunt-niece game, and because we're no longer getting off on it quite as easily, we let it get out of hand, we brought them, Samira and Jenna, into it, by way of an actual, not-pretend job interview. Using them without their consent. So wrong on so many levels.

I couldn't unsee us this way. How wrong they thought we were.

•

Stella was silent as we drove out of the city, until we were on
the highway, passing under road signs with the names of towns
she grew up around, and she said: *Shit.* She hadn't called in to
work, she was supposed to be there right now.

"Have they called you?" I asked.

"I don't know. I turned my phone off so I wouldn't have to
hear anything from Alice."

"I'm sure it'll be fine. You could tell them you had a family
emergency."

She shook her head again, it didn't matter. She didn't even
reach for her phone.

"What do you want to do?" I asked her. "We can do anything you want."

"I don't know," she said, and what she was really saying
was this: *I want to not want anything. Can you help me with
that?*

We were out of wine, I had downed our last bottle the night
of Alice in the kitchen. So I pulled into the lot of a liquor
store, a package store as they called it here. Stella got out of
the car with me and we went inside, up and down aisles of
worn linoleum and metal shelving lined with alcohol. I think
my father must have come to a place just like this one, which
couldn't have changed much over thirty, forty years, to buy the
liquor we brought to the woman in the housecoat, pink carpet

underfoot, one Christmas so long ago. I still didn't really know too much about liquor, or wine for that matter, but Stella had already put two bottles of Irish whiskey in a plastic shopping basket and she walked the aisle like she wasn't done. The man behind the counter—sunken-cheeked, a baked-on tan like he worked outdoors when he wasn't working here, early thirties maybe, scruffy, wolfish—eyed the two of us from under his baseball cap, separately then together, and he saw a half-dressed young woman whose haircut wasn't meant for him and a not-young woman in black clothes that weren't meant for him, and though none of this was meant for him, he also saw the aunt-niece thing we were up to, and unlike Samira and Jenna, he didn't care. He was into it. Maybe too into it. He'd come along with us if we invited him, maybe even if we didn't. His interest made me want to pay for our bottles and get the fuck out of there, while it also made me think it wouldn't be as easy as that. But then.

"Hey," Stella said to him at the register. She didn't know him personally, but she knew him as a type. "So, listen, this morning I found my girlfriend, who fucking goes to *Harvard*"—she laughed when she said *Harvard*—"with some bro-fuck named *Brian*"—that same laugh—"and then I basically killed my friend here's chance at getting a job and I'm probably gonna be fired from *my* job now. So do you think this'll be enough to get us properly shit-faced tonight?"

"Yeah, this'll do," he said. "And fuck that Harvard skank."

They gave each other smiling nods, a tribal sign. Stella had spoken to him with the local accent I thought she didn't have.

But of course she had it. Or could bring it back just like that. I had thought, when we met, that she sounded like she could be from anywhere. But nobody is from no place. Nobody real.

Sunk into the couch in the living room, Stella and I watched episode after episode of a reality show where the reality was that no one ever experienced emotional growth. Middle-aged women in tight, expensive jeans bickered, they gossiped, they got on private jets, they dermatologically enhanced themselves, they went to charity events, all while having the same conversation over and over again using different words and wearing different pairs of tight, expensive jeans. It was mesmerizing. And I wasn't even that drunk, though Stella was. One of the bottles of Jameson was more than half empty. We each had a corner of the couch, our feet skirting each other's in the center.

Stella hit pause, freeze-framing on a palm tree.

"I'm still wearing what I wore to bed last night," she said.

"It happens."

"What if I just wear this forever? If you don't take off your clothes, ever, do they eventually, like, merge with your skin?"

She lifted up her shirt from the neckline and looked down through it. Then, more intently, she sat straighter and leaned toward me. She lifted the hem of my shirtdress, grazing my thigh, and looked in. I pulled the collar of my shirtdress up to my eyes, like a black tent, a tunnel of dark, soft light, and I met her frank, unblinking gaze at the other end. But in doing so, I'd turned it into a game a child might play. She let her end drop and the light fell away. I wasn't supposed to have looked at her under my shirtdress. I was supposed to close my eyes, let my head lean against the armrest, let her hands move along my legs, let them push my dress up over my hips, let her mouth go wherever it wanted. She didn't want to see me, my face, she had only wanted to see Not Alice and I could have been Not Alice if I hadn't looked at her. But I made us see each other.

It made me think of something, flash on something, from a long time ago, that I both was and wasn't intimately involved in. The beach by the lake. At night. Berrie and John, and me and Stuart. John, with his lips that always seemed slightly parted, as if you'd caught him perpetually unawares, as if he didn't know why we girls looked at him the way we did, an innocence that offset his masculinity. Berrie with her gray eyes and husky, worldly voice, her eager smile. Stuart with his what? I didn't know anymore, I remembered Stuart mostly as a harmless, nondescript presence, which was terrible, but true. Berrie and John were kissing, more than kissing, John on top of Berrie, lying on a towel in the sand. Stuart and I were doing the same thing, only it felt like an approximation or an imitation of what Berrie and John were doing and not the real thing. Stuart and I were a more fully clothed, upside-down mirror image of Berrie and John: I was on top of Stuart, and we were behind Berrie and John on the sand, facing in the opposite direction so that when I happened to look up—why I looked up I'm not sure—I saw John looking directly at me. We locked eyes for what couldn't have been more than several seconds but the look didn't seem to adhere to temporality at all, until he made a sound like his breath caught and he shuddered into Berrie.

We never mentioned it to each other and I never mentioned it to Berrie. I had liked him looking at me while he was kissing her, while he was fucking her, it turned out, and if she knew he'd looked at me and that I liked it, we wouldn't have any more of those nights on the beach. We wouldn't have any more nights where it was just the two of us, either, Berrie and me, the whispering nights in our sweatshirts on the bunk steps after she sang "Taps," and the girls had gone to sleep.

What was it? A form of betrayal, despite the fact that John and I had never touched. Barely spoke. Never saw each other again after that summer. Berrie and I remained friends for a few years after we stopped going to camp and I never thought that, deep-down, I kept in touch with her because it was a way—a faithless, deceptive way—of holding on to what I felt when John and I locked eyes. Berrie and I drifted apart, eventually, without much ado or regret, and the intensity of that memory drifted, too. But still.

What if Berrie knew the whole time? What if even Stuart knew? What if they abided it because, however perversely, they got something out of it, too? Desire like shards of a mirror reflecting and refracting in endless combinations. And all of it inchoate, inarticulate, back then, at least.

Inarticulate still. If you spoke of it, it would disappear. You could get some diluted version of it, maybe, an agreement, an open understanding of needs and terms. All very adult and forthright, and everyone gets off and no one gets hurt. But what if the hurt, the thing no one wants to inflict and no one wants to feel and no one wants to talk about, is in some way, in some measure, necessary to all of it? David knew and Stella knew—not every detail, of course, though there must have been an awareness—and they'd abided it. I didn't want to hurt David, or Stella, or even myself, but we live on two levels all the time, the articulate and the inarticulate, and being here in this place, at Alder, I'd been submerged in the inarticulate, it seemed to me now, like the unconscious mind was a lake I'd been swimming in day after day. Where cause and effect, action and consequence, didn't work as they usually do. It wasn't an excuse; it's just the way it was.

I'd kept my head down in the blackness of my shirtdress, not seeing Stella's reaction, her possible disappointment or shame or revulsion, only feeling her shift back into her corner of the couch, hearing the TV come on again, the women in tight, expensive jeans picking up where they left off, the whiskey being poured into a glass.

I thought I heard the front door. David. If I hadn't looked at Stella through the tunnel of my dress, what would he have walked in on? Maybe nothing. Maybe I would have stopped Stella, told her I couldn't be Not Alice. Maybe she would have been frustrated but grateful later, sober. And if David had walked in on something, it would have been an ending, though I'm not sure I would have been able to explain that to him or if it would have mattered. There was enough to explain to him as it was. Early that morning, when we'd last seen each other, last checked in, Alice was out of the picture, our picture at any rate, Stella was becoming a kind of ghostly guest who made no demands, who left little impression beyond the tracks of her bike tires, and I was about to get a job—along with whatever money, security, status, and sense of self-worth that offered.

He stood in the archway between the hall and the living room, a little like a husband, a father, a man from an era of overcoats and cigarettes and unforgiving gender expectations, returning not simply from work but from a whole world so removed from the home he'd entered, from his family, domestic life. Stella had once been able to exist with him on this plane, the two of them like old friends, with some shared knowledge or history that made me feel remote—the image I'd had of them during the storm, when we'd taken Stella in. But I no longer knew what plane she was on, what plane any of us were on, really. It was the three of us in the room, as we'd been during the storm, but suddenly there were six of us, as if we'd doubled and our private, secret selves had emerged and were visible, occupying space. They were dressed just as we were. Our doubles looked at each other, acknowledged and took each other in, but they didn't say anything. David and his double sat down in an armchair, reached for the glass of whiskey my double and I weren't going to finish, and all six of us silently watched the women in tight, expensive jeans on the screen get on a yacht.

NECESSARY WAYS

"Maybe it's for the best," I said. "There are more meaningful ways to make a living. I could be doing something much more valuable with my time."

"Valuable to whom?" David asked.

"I don't know. Someone other than wealthy moms with nice taste and ethical shopping habits."

David was hunched over his knees, sitting on the edge of the wing chair in our room, a tired coach, still trying, out of habit, to motivate the players who had disappointed him. I sat on the floor, knees up, my arms around my shins.

"I understand why you went with Stella to find Alice," he said. "You thought she was in real trouble. I get that. But I don't really understand why you'd bring Stella with you to your interview. From a professional perspective."

"I wasn't thinking professionally, I guess. If you'd seen her . . . Stella. I mean, you wouldn't have left her alone in the car or wherever."

He wouldn't have, I was sure of it. Stella was downstairs on the couch. She'd fallen asleep sometime after the women disembarked from the yacht but before they convened later that day, in full evening regalia, at a philanthropic gala. David had placed a blanket over her, asked me to fill a glass of water and leave it on the coffee table for her. How caring, how thoughtful he was. How naturally it came to him.

"I don't know," he said.

"Yes, you do."

I thought of how he'd defended me, at our dinner party, to Liz. How he'd been my champion, and how I'd let him down, how I'd forgotten to be his champion, forgotten he might even need one or need me to be one, these last weeks, months, longer. He rubbed his hand wearily into the left side of his face and I got to my feet, so that I was no longer looking up at him from the floor, he was looking up at me from the chair.

"Have you really been working late these past few nights?" I asked, not as an accusation but as a form of self-recrimination. I hadn't been paying enough attention but I would make up for it. "I mean, when you've been late, have you been working?"

Yes, he nodded, not defensively, but sadly, almost gravely, with the understanding that it could have gone another way, if there had happened to be a Stella or an Alice, maybe, at his office. Or that he'd been working late because he did legitimately have work to do, but that the work also provided a good, convenient excuse to be elsewhere. Or that his working hard, for the both of us, coincided with a personal need of his that had little to do with the both of us. All of it, in that nod.

I was frightened by the thought that David would leave me. I didn't want to consider it much beyond supposing that if it were to actually happen, I could do something, in theory, about it. Figure out some action to take and take it. What frightened me in a different but more uncanny way was thinking: What if we had happened to meet at the wrong time, as he put it, and hadn't liked each other in the necessary way, and naively, stupidly, hadn't recognized who we might become to each other, with each other, and carelessly walked away? We'd worked for what we'd become, and in working we'd had some control over things, but the origin of it was so frighteningly flimsy, so arbitrary as to be destabilizing.

What if we hadn't learned how to read each other well and closely? A skill you may not always practice, but once picked up, like swimming or riding a bike, you don't forget. It comes back to you, to your body. So that when I said, "We need to sell this place," it wasn't a random thought I happened to land on, but the vocalization of a decision, a directive we had arrived at by the fact that we could still read each other, the proof of a certain complicity between us.

"And Stella?" he asked, because she'd become our responsibility. "Where does Stella go?"

I couldn't read him closely enough, though, to know how literally he meant this. David solved problems—David with the dead baby birds, lifting them on cards, carrying them away for burial—but Stella wasn't a problem to solve. She wasn't a baby bird that fell out of the nest. Logistics get figured out one way or another. There would be a new place, somewhere, somehow, for her to physically reside. But where would *she* go? And where would the event of her, in our lives, go now?

"We'll talk to her in the morning. It's going to take a while anyway, to figure it out and put it all in motion."

He yawned, an involuntary movement but willfully exaggerated, his eyes clenched shut, his jaw stretched as open as possible, exposing the dark silver fillings in two of his molars, deep into the cavity of his mouth, like a roaring elephant seal, but on mute. And then I yawned, too. It was contagious. How many thousands of times had one of us seen the other yawn and then responded in kind? An uncontrolled mimicry that has to do with empathy, or so I've read.

In the morning, a bright blue morning with a sharp coolness that signaled fall, the cotton blanket was neatly folded on the couch. The tumbler of water was washed and drying on the rack in the kitchen. And a note: *Thank you. S.*

David read a finality into it, that Stella had already gone for good. But I didn't think she would have left like that and I wanted my impression to be the right one, some indication that I understood Stella, that we understood each other in a way that David didn't fully comprehend. At the same time, I tried to hide any anxiousness from David. I didn't want to *be* anxious about the possibility of her not being there. No running to her bunk—I waited, and when I did make my way over that afternoon, I stopped myself before reaching her. It was enough to see her clothes still out there in the sun, hanging on the line.

HOURS, DAYS, AND YEARS

It had been Aunt Esther's proto-feminist desire to make Alder a camp for girls. And, from what I knew, what I saw or had been told, it had been Uncle Joe's desire to please Aunt Esther. He was invested in Alder, involved in the running of it, was a presence at camp-wide events. At athletic games, he consistently wore around his neck a black-and-gold lanyard with a whistle. He had a beautiful voice and for years he would sing Irving Berlin's "Always" at each end-of-summer banquet with the backing of a tape-recorded instrumental track, his eyes gleaming by the middle of it, because it wasn't, as it could so easily sound, a song about unconditional, unquestioning love; it was about love that acknowledged conditions and questions, that committed itself to existing within those conditions and questions. Joe was as sentimental as he was grouchy. (*What the fuck is wrong with people?*) He loved this place, but he loved it because of Esther, and if she had ever been done with it, he would have been, too. It wasn't that she dominated him and he submitted to her will. At least, it didn't look like that to me. What it looked like was two people who believed in each other.

They had done something unusual together. Two people who were fairly conventional in the way they dressed and carried themselves, the way they presented to the world. But they had, in some measure, rejected what had been expected of them and then had had to redefine and readjust what they'd expected of themselves.

After we lost the baby, I had days that felt directed by a kind of grasping compulsion, a monomania: *We will try again. We'll keep trying. Whatever it takes.* It was hearing myself say that—*whatever it takes*—that made me stop and wonder what did that even mean? *It takes too much. It takes something you don't have.* At what point does persistence turn into delusion? Maybe what I was operating under was neither persistence nor delusion but a kind of fever that eventually broke, around the time Aunt Esther left me Alder. *I couldn't keep losing*, I heard her say in my head.

When the fever broke, I'd asked David: How badly do you want a child?

Implicit in the question was another question, a sad, desperate one: Badly enough to leave me and go find someone else who can give you that life?

"I want," he'd said, "I wanted . . . I want a child with *you.* I don't even mean biologically. Maybe it's adoption. Or foster parenting. Or maybe it's something else. But whatever it is, I want it to be with you."

At our dinner party, David had talked about the creative impulse that brought us here. Joe and Esther would have understood that idea, I think. Esther hadn't left me Alder on a whim.

My instinct, when faced with all the old snapshots in the house, old papers and fading purple mimeographs in the administrative office at the lodge, the wall of yearbooks, was archaeological. I would never have thought to toss these artifacts. Or to let them go unnoticed. I wanted to unearth them, examine them, glean something from them. They were like clues that suggested a mystery. The point wasn't to solve the mystery, only to recognize it was there. I knew there was a chance I might discover something I didn't want to know about Esther, about Joe. But I never did. Which isn't to say they didn't have secrets—everyone does, even or especially from themselves. Only that I believed in the belief they had in each other. I never found anything that made me doubt it.

GOING UNDER

The lake had a different cast to it. A new stillness and clarity, the water like a mirror. The trees darkened, even in full sun. Stella sat out on a towel in the sand, in her black bikini, and didn't get up when she saw me coming toward the low wall, but she waved.

"Hi," she said.

"How are you?" I asked.

"I'm fine, I guess." She was leaning back on her hands, her long legs stretched out and crossed in front of her. I laid my own towel down and sat beside her.

"I wasn't sure if you'd be at work or—"

"I have today off. They didn't fire me, at the coffee shop." Her words sounded less like relief and more like regret. She hadn't lost her job; instead, she had to do it forever now.

"That's good," I said, wanting to say something better, something more reflective of her tone, of some understanding between us. "I mean . . ."

"No, it is good, to have a place to go, to have to show up and be somewhere."

And she pulled back a little, as if she, in turn, had said the wrong thing, remembering that I still didn't have a place to be. Aside from this place, which wouldn't be for much longer. I decided to tell her at that moment—there would never be a right time—that I'd spoken to a real estate agent over the weekend. That David and I were looking for someone with experience in this kind of process, who would hopefully help us secure a worthy buyer who could do what we couldn't: bring this place to life again. Though, it occurred to me, my eyes landing on her blue painted nails, fanned out behind her, we did bring it to life, in a way.

I told Stella she could stay here, as long as she wanted, until a sale went through. She appeared to take the news pretty stoically. It wasn't entirely unexpected, after all. And what more did I want from her? For her to be distressed by this development, for her to need comforting? From me?

"You want to go for a last swim, then?" She pointed to the water.

"It's not like it's happening tomorrow."

"No, but—" She didn't finish the thought. She stood up and headed onto the dock and I followed her to the two inflatable plastic donuts sitting out there and we tossed them in before diving in their direction. The water was the warmest it had been all summer and we floated. We floated until the sky was full of low steel-gray clouds, and our fingers, dangling in the water, had wrinkled.

We gathered our things and walked in the drizzling rain, past the old infirmary, the steps where we'd kissed, an experience that had already become part of the past—like Stella sitting in the infirmary the day she came to work with her mother, or me lying inside there years before that as a feverish girl in a hot-pink T-shirt—the way everything here became part of the past, how it all seemed to get subsumed. To become a buried ruin that might never be excavated.

Inside the house, we changed into dry clothes. I took the towels to the wash and then found her in the living room, by the cabinet with the TV.

"What is this?"

"It's a VCR."

"I know, I was kidding."

She crouched and started going through a cardboard box on the floor, marked "videos"—a box I'd kept long after my own VCR broke and despite the fact that I never bought another machine. But Aunt Esther had one in working order, of course. So I'd brought the box out when we'd arrived and had been making my way through them once again. Stella picked up a copy of *Summer*, what Rohmer's *Le Rayon Vert* was called when it was released in America.

"This looks appropriate," she said.

"I haven't seen that one in a long time. It was going to be next."

"Well then."

She pushed the cartridge in and we were back on the couch, in our places from before, but neither of us said a word about what had happened then, her looking up my shirtdress, me looking back at her, whether she thought I'd refused her or she'd refused me.

On screen appeared Delphine: young, single, lonely, brunette, French, working as a secretary, restless and dislocated one summer. She's a downer. Her friends don't want to vacation with her. She doesn't fit. In her own skin, even. She talks to a table full of incredulous meat-eaters about being a vegetarian, how lettuce is like a friend. Her self-consciousness makes you cringe, for her, for yourself—the cringing is a kind of recognition of all the mistakes and all the necessary self-deceptions of a certain age. Of any age, maybe. People like to think it disappears along with youth, but I'm not sure it really ever does. I kept wondering if Stella was finding the movie insufferable, slow, arty, but she just watched it and watched it. By the end, when Delphine, at the edge of the ocean, with, finally, a *sportif*, understanding young man, witnesses the rare green flash above the setting sun and gasps, it seems like everything has led up to that gasp. Delphine is a romantic, holding out for something that exists but is as uncommon, as extraordinary as that solar phenomenon, and if you discount or deride her romantic nature, her longings, you do so out of some smallness in yourself, you do so at your own risk. Stella was pulled into herself, knees to her chin, biting the pad of her thumb. She wasn't teary but something was welling up, something she tried to hold back with her teeth.

Minor-key strings, credits.

"What did you think?" I asked dumbly.

She was half in the world of the movie, half on the couch in the room with me.

"I don't want to be that guy," she said, out loud but almost to herself. I wasn't sure who she meant. The *sportif* young Frenchman?

"What guy?"

"The guy in the liquor store, behind the counter, when we were buying the whiskey. I don't want to be some version of him someday. The guy who grew up around here and never leaves. I know that sounds snobby, but I just don't want that and I'm not sure how I get out of it."

Alice had gotten her out of it, for a time, but Alice was gone. Whatever door Alice opened had now closed. I wanted to say to Stella: *Come with us*, and I wanted to mean it. I wanted impossible things. I wanted to say to her *You'll get out of it* but I didn't know how to make those words not sound empty.

"Look," I said, "I don't know that guy. You don't really know that guy, what his story is. But I do know you're not that guy. You're already not that guy and you never were that guy."

Her eyelids fluttered as they closed, as if anesthesia were kicking in, and when she opened them again, her stoicism from before was back.

"David will be home soon," she said. Asked.

"Probably."

"I should get going."

I wanted to say: *No, you don't have to.* But I couldn't and she did, have to.

OPPORTUNITY

I didn't immediately recognize the name, Denise Taylor. Who was she and why did I have an email from her? Was she a real estate agent? A paralegal? But then it occurred to me that she was replying to an email I'd sent her. Denise Taylor, the executive director of the film foundation I'd worked at so many summers ago. Denise Taylor! Whom I'd contacted out of the blue, in the hush of the house, after that dazed afternoon with Alice and Stella, in the pickup truck, at the Thai restaurant, at the lake. I'd written to her but it had felt more like I was using semaphore or Morse code with an unknown communicant, trying to convey a message to someone who may not have known how to read it or, more likely, wasn't even there. Not entirely pointless, but not particularly productive either. But Denise had picked up on what I'd put out. And she'd responded, with a long block of text that brought her back to me in a way her short bio and poorly lit picture on the foundation's website never did. Denise, you were a filmmaker, you knew about light, so why the shitty photo? Because you were no longer a filmmaker? You started out as a documentarian; you made a prizewinning feature in the late '80s about women and AIDS. But you stopped for some reason, and your work, for the larger part of your life, had become mostly administrative and organizational.

Denise from Queens. Richmond Hill. You came to Boston for school and surprised yourself by never returning to New York, not to live, anyway. "You can take the girl out of Queens," you once said. "But you can't take Queens out of the girl," Nick had finished, in the voice of a two-bit comedian. To which you drily replied, "No, Nick. Just the first part. I'm no longer in Queens." And you looked at me, the intern, and your eyes said: *This guy. Guys in general. Fucking men.* And I probably thought, *But he gave me his shirt!* If you'd known what I thought, you would have shaken your head and gently smiled. *He gave you his shirt. Big fucking deal.*

Denise: your limp black hair, flat face, olive complexion, brass bracelets accentuating the lean, ropey muscularity of your arms, always in oversized button-down shirts, sleeves rolled, or black bodysuits, mascara. But that was nearly twenty years ago. In the shitty picture your skin was sallow, your torso thicker, your hair wiry, silver, your eyes disappeared into the flat plane of your face.

I think Denise came back to me so clearly just then

because I could see myself becoming her, the ways in which I already had.

How nice to hear from you! she wrote. Yes, of course she remembered me, after all this time. How could she forget the girl who lugged that sack of bulk mail when "that asshole Nick couldn't be bothered to do it himself." She continued: "God, what a dick." As I might have been aware, the organization had experienced its share of ups and downs—"as we all do, right?"—but they seemed to have found a good, stable home, in somewhat different form, within their current academic setting. In some bittersweet news, she noted, she'd be leaving, retiring at the end of the year. There would be some reshuffling of their small staff and they'd need an administrative assistant, a very entry-level position to start, but with a lot of potential. "And I promise, no heavy lifting, haha!" Perhaps I knew someone who might be interested?

IN TIME

David pulls the collar up on his coat as we walk, along the path of a city park not too far from our apartment. George, our dog, doesn't strain the leash—the volunteer who cared for him at the shelter called him a "mellow fellow"—but he sets our pace. It's December, late afternoon on a Saturday, and a chilly mist clings to the trees, to the classical stone statuary by the pond, our faces. The days get dark early but the evenings glow with holiday lights. *Yeah, seasons*, I think, as Alice once said, and it makes me laugh. Because seasons, as she would have had it, are a marketing concept but they also exist, here, at least for now, and I haven't forgotten Alice. David asks what's funny and I don't know where to begin, how to tell a private joke you have with your own past. And I don't even really know what's funny about it anyway.

"Just something that happened at work," I say. But then I can't come up with anything that happened at work quick enough and the pretense collapses. I clumsily unravel the whole thought process to David until we're talking about how you can't really talk to someone else about private jokes with your own past. The setup is so long and convoluted, the punch line so paltry and unsatisfying. But as we talk, as Alice, Stella, our old house, and that summer come up into conversation, they seem like allusions to a past that we, and only we, shared.

It makes me think of something Liz told me, while she and Felix were separated. That it was so weird, fraught, difficult to speak to each other, at first especially, but they had to speak in order to talk about their kids, and when they talked about their kids, they spoke a language exclusive to themselves.

"No one else cares about your kids in the same way," she said. I took that to mean that while other people cared about her children's well-being, empathetically or ethically, nobody else delighted so completely in Valeria learning to raise her eyebrows, using her whole face, practically, to do it. Or Abigail, in pants that were now too short for her, concluding that she must be going through a "life burst" when she meant "growth spurt." Nobody else felt their own heart trampled when a group of kids refused to let Valeria join their playground game. Or when Abigail found out she hadn't been invited to a sleepover at her "best" friend's house and she didn't cry, she only grew quiet and withdrawn.

"You can bore me with the details," I'd said. "If you can't talk to Felix."

"That's just it," she'd replied. "I'd be boring you. I'm bored by other people's kids. It's pretty boring when they're not yours. Felix is the only other person who will always want to know these things about the girls and will never be bored by hearing them."

I'm not Felix, but I like that Liz tiptoes around me less and less when it comes to talking about her children, about parenthood. I like that she doesn't have to. That, somehow, I'm no longer baring a wound she can't care for.

George lets out a low, groaning warble, his "I'm done here, let's go home" sound. A mostly greyhound mutt, he's generally quiet, though he howls or roos sometimes in response to other dogs in the park or on the street, sometimes if we sing to him. We'd never had a pet before George, though David had grown up with retrievers. When we first brought George home, we'd set out a dog bed for him, but he spent every night curled up by David, until he eventually switched to the foot of our bed, between the both of us. At the shelter, he'd looked bedraggled, like he'd seen a lot, and beseeching: *Please take me with you.* So we did.

There's no equivalency—a dog is not a child. I don't mean to suggest we even thought about George in those terms, as an antidote to an absence. But George looks at me with such intelligence, such comprehension, and I look at him with so much love, and if I tried to tell anyone but David much more about it, I'd bore them so fast.

•

The next day, Sunday, I go with Liz and her children to see *The Nutcracker*. Liz has thoughts, from a professional, critical standpoint, about the ballet, the dancers, the staging, and the limitations of tradition. "But, fuck it," she says, and we mill about with a crowd of all ages in the opulent lobby of the theater, removing our gloves and hats and scarves by a marble column, beneath a chandelier. The lights flicker and Valeria, seven, grabs her mother's hand while Abigail, nine, takes mine, as if she's doing it, kindly, for my benefit. The kind of nine-year-old who reads books with young heroines and seeks out acts of compassion wherever she can. We head into the performance hall, which was built to be a palace of sorts: gold leaf and ornate plasterwork, row upon row of deep red seats from which you might lift your gaze heavenward toward the celestial murals on the ceiling. The music begins, the curtain comes up on a beautiful party, a giant mouse does battle with a militarized kitchen gadget, essentially, and a girl and a prince travel through the Realm of Snow to the Land of Sweets. I hadn't seen it in full since I was around Abigail's age. As a child, I might have understood on some level that the ordinary reality, the point of departure for this imaginary adventure, is a bourgeois family of four: mother, father, two children. But it strikes me now, thinking of Liz's bourgeois family of four, that this reality is itself a fantasy, made real enough. Felix is back at home, he and Liz are still married, but when they separated for a while and Felix moved out, Liz slept with a carpenter, a professor, and a pharmacist. I don't know who Felix slept with. Nobody, ultimately, who could infiltrate his marriage and the life it predicated. I look at Abigail and Valeria and wonder how they will remember that time when things weren't as they ordinarily are. If it will come back to them, vivid but half-understood, like condensation on the windows of a room with pink walls and pink carpeting, porcelain plates hung as decoration, and a woman in a housecoat. They'll ask Liz or Felix what was happening but their parents won't remember or they'll remember it on their own terms, which don't include a room or a woman like that, and the girls will begin to confuse what was real with what they dreamed.

Outside the theater it's already night, black and clear. A glow from the street lamps, the marquee. It's not late, not even five, but that Sunday feeling is setting in. Today has been an excursion, a trip to the city for Valeria and Abigail, who live in a modest house in a near-suburb. Valeria wore brightly striped leggings, Abigail her favorite purple corduroys. They say— Abigail says and Valeria seconds—they don't want to go home yet, they want to get on the T, come home with me. A slumber party is a great idea, I tell them, but we need to plan for it. Not tonight, but soon, I say. In a week, they'll be on school vacation, right? Maybe then. And I mean it. Valeria doesn't yet have a real sense of time, of its passing, but Abigail does. She already understands herself, in some incipient way, as moving through it. Wanting to remember. She saves her program from the performance, while Valeria's lies forgotten somewhere under a seat, probably, in the theater. Abigail is the protagonist of her own story. (And maybe this is why Liz is ultimately half-right: Valeria, as someone else's child, bores me after a while.

Abigail, as her own person, does not.) I suppose I'm a supporting character in Abigail's story. She doesn't call me "Aunt Emily" but I think of my relationship with Aunt Esther. And I can imagine that, when the time comes, if I have something to leave, I could leave it to her.

On the train, home to David, to George, I can see my reflection in the window by my seat. The fluorescent light in here is harsh but somehow, in the glass, I don't see that deepening vertical crease between my eyebrows that would indicate I'd done a good deal of frowning in my life. I turn away, look at the program I'm still holding in my lap, not because I continue to save these things but because I unthinkingly kept it in my hand and now I can't recycle it until I get home. I flip through the pages of head shots and bios, what I always do with these things, even though it undoes the spell of the performance. It's like they don't want the spell to last. They draw a line, create a frame around it, that reminds you not to confuse a dream with what is real. Who do I even mean by *they*?

And what was real? I still have Stella in my phone. Though maybe I don't, maybe what I have is now a number for someone else. I haven't tried it in months, I think, and then I realize that those months have turned into more than three years. From time to time—Denise Taylor must have added me to the mailing list before she stepped down or stepped back, retired—I receive a newsletter from the film foundation. Programming notes, updates on educational outreaches, fund-raising events. Stella Dart is listed as the contact for more information. She's in Boston, in the position that I recommended her for, or some greater, expanded version of it. I might look up one day and see her on the train. I could get in touch with her, but I never do. I'm not sure if she even writes these email communications but I read them that way, as communications from her. They sound like her. Not ironic or glib, but playful somehow. Unassuming but smart. Considered but not mannered. I remember talking to her, whenever I read these dispatches, whether she writes them or not. Conversations return to me. Her voice. *Who the fuck has a passion for juices? Oh my god, Alice! How can it not be personal? It's like, I do my job and I don't give a shit but I do give a shit. Gimme my shirt, lady. Why though? Why should she?*

It was Alice's voice that I heard in my head yesterday. But mostly, when that summer at Alder comes to me, it comes in images, sensations, movements. One pear, halved, on the cutting board, a shaft of light through the window, hitting the kitchen table. The green aluminum of the dock and the blue-black lake. Rafters and floorboards. Gasoline and cut grass. Laundry drying on a line. Stella pulling a couple of shirts and a pair of jeans off clothespins along with a bedsheet, white and glinting in the sun. We could be women in a Mediterranean country, a century ago, doing the wash, carrying baskets. We just happened to find ourselves here, pulling to the corners of the sheet, coming together and moving back, in a kind of dance, until there's no more fabric to fold.

ACKNOWLEDGMENTS

Thank you to Kate Garrick and Jonathan Lee for the extraordinary care and attention you've given this book. I'm incredibly fortunate to work with you. I'm grateful to everyone at Catapult for all the tremendous support. Maryse Meijer and Carlene Bauer, I owe you endlessly. Thank you also to Rebecca Shapiro, Rita Zilberman, Carole Obedin, Elizabeth Stigler, and Alison Hart. And to Lewis and Callum, where would I even start?